D

SIX-GUN SHOWDOWN

The riders came from the north, six of them. Jim Casey saw them coming, and he saddled his horse and made himself visible. They stopped and talked among themselves, looking his way. Casey checked the long-barreled rifle, raised the trap door, and shoved a round into the firing chamber.

One of the riders waved his hat and hollered something. The wave was supposed to be a friendly gesture, but Jim didn't trust them. He let them ride closer and then, holding the reins in his left hand, he fired a shot in the air, hoping to discourage them. The horse snorted and jerked back, but didn't pull free. The riders stopped again, talked among themselves.

Suddenly they drew six-guns, spurred their horses, and charged straight at Casey, firing as they came.

DOYLE TRENT

DEVIL'S DISCIPLE

ZEBRA BOOKS
KENSINGTON PUBLISHING CORP.

ZEBRA BOOKS are published by

Kensington Publishing Corp.
475 Park Avenue South
New York, NY 10016

Zebra and the Z logo Reg. U.S. Pat & TM Off.

First Printing: December, 1993

Printed in the United States of America

Chapter One

The prosecuting attorney raved on, words spewing out of his mouth like water from a pump. In his opening statement, he called James B. Casey every kind of vile name there was. His favorite name was Land Baron, which he used interchangeably with Cattle Baron. His favorite adjective was greedy.

He told the jury how Casey, in his never-ending quest for more land, had driven off homesteaders, bought off others at half what their land was worth, accused the honest, hardworking farmers of grand theft, dammed the creeks and hogged the water, and now . . . now came the most heinous crime of all.

Defense attorney Amos P. Sharp patted Casey on the arm and whispered, "Don't worry, we'll have our turn."

Casey was worried, but he tried not to show it. While the prosecutor raved, he looked each of the twelve jurors in the eye, one at a time. Each juror sneaked only quick glances at him. Most of them were farmers, homesteaders. Among the others were laborers at the barrel factory, a clerk in the Howell Mercantile, and a hostler at the freight yards.

Amos P. Sharp had used all his peremptory challenges, trying to seat jurors who had no opinion one way or the other of the defendant. But that was next to impossible. The defendant owned more land than any man ought to and more cattle than he could keep track of. This in a county where most folks were either starving out and moving on or were barely scratching out a living.

Attorney Sharp had moved for a change of venue, but the deputy district attorney had argued that the motion was only a delaying tactic and the trial should be conducted speedily and in the county where the crime was committed. Judge Harold J. Buckley had waggled his thick gray eyebrows and denied the motion.

"We will prove," the prosecutor went on now, "that the defendant had a very strong motive for this crime. We will prove that his motive was pure greed. We will prove that he was overheard exchanging heated words with the deceased, words that were not only harsh, but also threatening."

"Oh no," Casey whispered to Amos P. Sharp. "Harsh, yes, threatening, no."

"Don't worry," the defense attorney whispered. "I shall cross-examine every witness relentlessly."

"We will prove beyond a shadow of a doubt," the prosecutor said, "that the defendant was seen near the scene of the crime shortly before the crime was committed, and we shall produce a witness who saw a man fitting the defendant's description hastily leaving the scene."

The words stung, and Casey couldn't help squirming in his wooden chair at the defense table in what passed for the Oak County courthouse. But he kept his head up and his eyes fixed on the faces of the jurors, daring them to look him in the eye. None accepted his dare.

"Don't worry," Amos P. Sharp whispered.

"Gentlemen of the jury," the deputy DA said, pausing

at exactly the right moments to be sure each word sunk in, "we will prove that one James B. Casey did for his own personal gain, in cold blood, with malice afterethought, shoot and kill the beloved Reverend John Weems." With that, the young deputy DA wiped his flushed round face with a polka-dot handkerchief, and dropped into his chair at the prosecution table.

"Mr. Sharp?" the judge said, looking over his pince-nez glasses at the defense attorney.

But before Amos P. Sharp could push his chair back and get to his feet, the deputy DA jumped up and exclaimed, "Your Honor, owing to the unnecessary length of time it took to seat a jury, it is now approaching five P.M. I move that we recess until nine A.M. tomorrow."

"Your Honor." Attorney Sharp buttoned his coat as he stood. "I believe I should be allowed my opening statement before the recess."

"Your Honor, most of the gentlemen on the jury are farmers who have chores to do, cows to milk and livestock to feed. It would work a hardship on members of the jury to continue this trial beyond five P.M."

"Mr. Sharp," District Court Judge Harold J. Buckley wore a severe, no-nonsense expression, "how much time do you need for your opening statement?"

"Well, Your Honor, I do want to point out some facts that I think the jury should keep in mind throughout the trial. My worthy opponent has made some untrue remarks that simply must be rebutted."

"A half-hour? An hour?"

"Probably close to an hour, Your Honor."

"Very well, this trial will resume at nine o'clock in the morning." *Bang,* went the judge's gavel.

"Don't worry," Amos P. Sharp said to his client.

* * *

But Jim Casey did worry. He was quiet as he rode back to his C Bar Ranch headquarters. Most of what the prosecutor had said was true. He owned more cattle than he could keep track of, and he held patent to eighty sections of foothills grassland. He grazed his cattle on at least a hundred square miles of public domain. True, he did buy land from homesteaders at half what he'd had to pay for government land, and he did dam a section of Pine Creek to irrigate some hayland.

But greedy? That depended on who was doing the talking.

Everything he owned he and Boots had earned. They'd started with a small inheritance from her side of the family and the proceeds from the sale of his late folks' farm. They'd worked from dawn to dark, fought Indians, traded shots with rustlers, froze in the winter, sweated in the summer, and built the C Bar into a big cow outfit.

A lot was going through Jim Casey's mind as he rode.

"They ain't heard our side of the story yet," Levi said quietly. "That lawyer, Amos Sharp, seems to know what he's doin'."

"Yeah."

They rode side by side on the wagon road that ran between Jack's Corners, next to the railroad, and the town of Rockledge. When they turned onto the C Bar road, which was nothing more than wagon ruts, Levi cleared his throat and spoke again:

"I know you didn't do it, and I'll testify. You and me was on our way back to the rancho when that preacher was killed."

"Yeah, but you work for me, and the DA will accuse you of lying for your employer."

"The other boys, there was two of 'em in the

bunkhouse, they know when we got back. And Miz Carter, she knows."

"Sure, but Reverend Weems had to have been shot before we were a mile out of town. The jury will think I shot him and we jumped on our horses and headed for home on a gallop."

Levi, the only name anyone knew him by, was fencepost lean, six feet tall, middle seventies, with a long skinny neck and an Adam's apple that bobbed when he talked. He pushed back his floppy black hat and squinted across the rolling hills on the east side of the Rocky Mountains. "There's gotta be some way we can prove you didn't do it."

"The only way I know is to find out who did. And the sheriff, he's so damned sure I'm the guilty one he isn't even looking for more clues."

"Well hell, Jim, gawddammit, there's gotta be a way."

"Yeah."

It was five miles, by most guesses, to the C Bar headquarters, and the sun was still an hour and a half above the Front Range mountains when they rode within sight of the buildings. The house was seven rooms, two-story, built of good lumber hauled from Denver. It had a split shingle roof, a hardwood floor, and a good rock foundation. But Casey remembered, as he rode closer, how he and Boots had lived the first thirteen years in a one-room log cabin with a tarpaper roof and a dirt floor.

Casey's eyes went to the grave under a stand of pines uphill from the house. Murdered by Cheyennes. Maybe even the same Indians she'd once fed. That's the way Boots was. It grieved her to see anything go hungry, even the savages.

Greedy? Not Mrs. Lucille Casey, nicknamed Boots because, from childhood, she liked to wear riding boots.

9

Muttering under his breath, Casey swore, "No, by God, and if that damned lawyer uses that word one more time I'm gonna knock his goddam head off and poke it up his dying ass."

"What'd you say, Jim?"

"Aw, nothing."

Amos P. Sharp was an orator, and he had a captive audience. In his opening statement, he reminded the jury that they were fortunate to be living in a free enterprise economic system. That it was a system which depended on entrepreneurship, and a willingness to work hard and take a gamble. The investors could lose everything as well as earn a profit, and more often than not they lost. He waved his right hand to the east and used the railroad, which now crossed Colorado from north to south, as an example of how the investors and planners had made life easier for nearly everyone. He told the jurors that it was no sin nor crime for an investor to make a profit, and the true entrepreneurs were the men who worked hard and reinvested their profits to make their business ventures grow.

He talked on until men in the jury section were squirming uncomfortably in their wooden chairs. The spectators who filled the room were beginning to mutter. Jim Casey was becoming exasperated.

Going back into history, the lawyer used Karl Marx and his doctrine as an example of how, in a socialist society, the shiftless and worthless element shared equally in everything produced by the hardworking and thrifty.

"Yes, gentlemen of the jury, you are very fortunate indeed to be Americans and allowed to profit from your labors." The lawyer turned his gaze toward Jim Casey.

"Now we have Mr. James B. Casey, who, with his late wife Lucile, are true entrepreneurs. Through their hard work and reinvestments, they have built a fine cattle ranch . . ."

Finally, Jim Casey thought, he's getting around to me. Maybe now he'll have something to say in my defense.

But now the jurors were restless, uncomfortable, wishing the orator would shut up. Three were gazing at the rafters in the warehouse which had been converted into a temporary courthouse. The other three were fighting to stay awake. Spectators were leaving.

Concluding with, "And we shall prove, gentlemen of the jury, that James B. Casey has absolutely nothing to be ashamed of and has committed no crime whatsoever," Amos Sharp unbuttoned his coat and sat.

The trial went on for two days. The deputy DA produced witnesses who told how Mr. Casey had paid only a pittance for land that homesteaders had worked for years to prove up on, how he'd tried to keep homesteaders away from public lands that he used as his own, how he'd falsely accused the less fortunate of stealing his cattle, and how he'd finally gone too far by closing, permanently, the mouth of a fine, God-fearing man who'd had the courage to speak out against him.

"It was greed, pure greed, that . . ."

He didn't get to finish what he was saying. Jim Casey jumped up so suddenly he knocked his chair over. He ran around the table intending to get his hands on that mealymouthed lawyer. The judge banged his gavel. Spectators yelled. The deputy DA scurried to the other side of the prosecution's table. Casey went after him, wanting to beat that round face into a bloody pulp. *Bang, bang,* went the judge's gavel.

"Order. Order."

Casey almost had him. Stretching across the table, he

got his fingertips on the lawyer's coat. But before he could strengthen his hold, arms grabbed him from behind. Two spectators held him back, while the prosecutor scurried behind the judge's high bench.

"Order."

"Please, Jim," Amos Sharp yelled above the turmoil, "sit down. Sit down, please. We'll have our say. Calm down. Sit down."

The courtroom was a madhouse. Jurors were standing, spectators were yelling and waving their hands. A deputy sheriff was behind Casey with an arm around his throat while two spectators held him by the arms. Old Levi got into the battle and hauled one of the spectators off his employer. He was punched in the face and knocked away, but he only blinked and jumped back into the middle of the struggle.

Judge Buckley yelled above the racket, "Mr. Sharp, instruct your client to take his seat. Mr. Casey, if you do not sit down and keep quiet I will have you bound and gagged."

"Please Jim, this isn't helping our defense. Please sit down."

It was hopeless, Casey knew. The insulting lawyer was cowering behind the judge's bench, and there were too many men between them. He saw Levi wrestling with the deputy sheriff, and knew the older man couldn't win either. He stopped fighting and said, "Levi, don't."

All struggling ceased. Judge Buckley banged his gavel again and shouted, "Will you all take your seats. Any more outbursts and the defendant will be bound and the courtroom will be cleared."

Levi and Deputy Sheriff Orville Rankin were scowling at each other. "You interfered with an officer of the law," the deputy growled.

"Shove your goddam law."
"I'll attend to you later."
"Please, Jim, please sit down."
After a while, the trial went on.

Chapter Two

The town of Rockledge was quiet, dying on its feet, until the Reverend Weems was murdered and the wealthiest man in the county was charged with the murder. That gave the citizens something to talk about besides the weather and the railroads.

Now there was a trial, the first trial ever held in the new county, and the citizens could talk of nothing else. Then the medicine show came to town.

A brightly painted red and white wagon with high sides and a canvas top was parked in front of the bank on First Street, and a calliope called to everyone within three miles.

Fortunately for the citizens, who couldn't be in two places at one time, Dr. Abraham kept the calliope quiet and his beautiful daughter out of sight while the trial went on. Not because the judge had sent the sheriff out to order him to, but because he didn't want to compete with the trial for attention.

The doctor was phony, but apparently only two people in Rockledge knew it. Dr. Benjamin Woodrow knew it. So did Hiram Samuels, who mixed drugs with mortars and pestles in a corner of the Howell Mercantile to fill prescriptions written by Dr. Woodrow. As disgusting as the phony doctor was, Dr. Woodrow kept it to himself. It would have been unprofessional for one doctor to criticize another. But after many years of study at King's College in New York and after two years of internship in New York hospitals, Dr. Woodrow couldn't help feeling a deep revulsion when he listened to the phony doctor tout his Chief Red Hawk's Elixer. It was a sure cure for everything, including female disorders, bilious colic, nervous derangement, and—Dr. Abraham dropped his voice an octave when he said it—loss of manhood.

An age-old Indian medicine, indeed. The main ingredient was whiskey. Cheap whiskey. Of course. When nothing better was available, whiskey was an antiseptic, anesthetic, pain killer, and courage-builder. A patient who drank enough of it—at a dollar a bottle—felt no pain for a while.

And it was unconscionable to use the girl, a beautiful blond goddess, to pose prettily and do pirouettes on the platform that unfolded from the side of the wagon, as a picture of perfect health and a living testament to the qualities of Chief Red Hawk's Elixer.

Dr. Woodrow readily admitted to himself that she was a picture of good health. And she was beautiful. But he attributed that to good genes. Certainly not to the quack doctor's phony Indian medicine.

Oh well, Dr. Woodrow had patients to attend to, and he had to testify in a murder trial. As the only doctor in over thirty miles, he doubled as the county coroner, and it was he who signed the death certificates for the deceased.

The jury paid close attention as he took the oath and sat in the witness chair. He was a good-looking man, in his late twenties, average build, with thick dark hair parted in the middle and a pleasant face. He wore a

15

white shirt with a high, stiff collar, and a cravat. Though the lawyers had discarded their formal coats in the too-warm courtroom, he kept his wool coat on. A professional man should look professional when he could.

"Now then, Dr. Woodrow, you have testified that the deceased died of a bullet wound in the heart. Do you have any way of knowing what caliber the bullet was?"

"No, I'm afraid not. The lead had struck the breast-bone and the lead and bone were both badly shattered."

"Do you have any way of knowing how close the murderer was to the deceased?"

"There were powder burns around the bullet wound."

"Then the murderer had to have been holding the gun very close."

"I know nothing of firearms. All I can say is there were powder burns around the wound. Also—"

"By that," interrupted the deputy DA, "we can ascertain that the weapon was held within two feet, and perhaps even closer than that, do you agree?"

Dr. Woodrow crossed his ankles and shook his head. "As I said, I know nothing about firearms. I also noticed—"

"That's all, doctor." The prosecutor turned his back on the witness.

"I might add that—"

Again, the witness was interrupted, this time by the judge. "Is there any cross-examination, Mr. Sharp?"

Standing, Amos Sharp answered, "None, Your Honor."

"The witness may step down."

Half-turning, facing the judge, Dr. Woodrow said, "Your Honor, I don't know whether this is pertinent, but—"

"Step down, please, Doctor."

Sheriff Waltham Jackson, stout, red faced, always

16

sweating, was next. He said the gun had to have been held close to leave powder burns.

"Were there any signs of a struggle?"

"No there wasn't."

"Would you surmise, then, that the murderer was known to the deceased and was able to just walk up and shoot him?"

"That could be."

Amos P. Sharp started to object, but changed his mind.

"It has been shown here, Sheriff Jackson, that the Reverend Weems and the defendant were acquainted, although certainly not friends."

No answer. None was expected. Again, Attorney Sharp started to object and changed his mind. There was no cross-examination, and the witness stepped down.

Then came the most damaging witness, Mrs. Agnes Mooreman, the widow Mooreman. She carried her forty-year-old body with dignity, head up, as she took the oath and the witness chair. Her wrinkle-free face was attractive with good features, and her dark hair was pulled back in a respectable bun. "A-hem," she cleared her throat.

She said she was with the good reverend in his rectory two days before the murder, and Mr. Casey came in and stood with his hand on the butt of his revolver, which was in a holster hanging from his belt on his right hip. Mr. Casey accused the reverend of telling lies about him and demanded to know why. When the reverend replied that he was telling the truth to his congregation, Mr. Casey appeared to be very angry. Mr. Casey went to the door and jerked it open, then turned to the good reverend and said, "You'd better be careful what you preach. Liars deserve to be shot."

At the defense table, Casey whispered, "Huh-uh. I

didn't say anything threatening. And I didn't have my hand on my gun."

"Don't worry."

But the defense lawyer couldn't get Mrs. Mooreman to change her story. He did get her to admit that she couldn't remember word for word everything said between the two men, but she remembered clearly that Mr. Casey was threatening.

"Are you certain about that?"

Her chin came up. "Yes sir."

Casey whispered, "She's lying."

"Mrs. Mooreman, you are a religious woman, are you not?" Without waiting for an answer, Lawyer Sharp went on, "Would you swear on the Holy Bible that Mr. Casey threatened to shoot Reverend Weems?"

For a second, Casey thought he had her, but only for a second. Her answer was hesitant, but easily understood, "Yes sir, I would."

With a shrug of resignation, the lawyer dropped into his chair at the defense table. "That's all."

Old Levi was next. He gave his name as Levi.

"What is your last name, sir?"

"Levi."

"Well, then, what is your first name?"

"Levi."

"Are we to believe that your full name is Levi Levi?"

Adam's apple bobbing, Levi said, "Yassir."

Grinning inwardly, Casey remembered how old Levi had refused to mention any other name, and how Boots had sometimes teased him by calling him Levi Levi.

Levi testified that he and Jim Casey did walk near the rectory where the Reverend Weems's body was found, but they did not go in. In fact, they went to their horses behind the Gold Dust Saloon and went back to the C Bar Ranch. On cross-examination, he said yes, he did work for Mr. Casey and Mr. Casey paid his wages.

"How much is he paying you to testify here?"

Then Levi was on his feet, shaking a work-gnarled finger at the prosecutor. "That's a durned insult and if you insult me again I'm gonna whip your sorry ass 'till you bark like a fox."

Bang, went the judge's gavel. Attorney Sharp jumped to his feet.

"Your Honor, the prosecution is deliberately badgering the witness."

"Sit down, Mr., uh, Levi. Mr. Prosecutor, you will refrain from badgering the witness." To the jurors he said, "The jury will disregard that question."

A smirk on his face, the prosecutor sat down. Regardless of the judge's instructions to the jury, he'd gotten his point across.

Amos Sharp didn't put his client on the witness stand, knowing he'd have to admit he was agitated with the reverend, and that they'd exchanged angry words. When the jurors glanced at the defendant, they saw a clean-shaved man forty-five years old, average height and build, with gray eyes, a wide mouth, and a strong chin. Jim Casey had sun wrinkles around his eyes, and enough brown hair left to part on the right side.

By mid-afternoon on the second day, both the prosecution and the defense rested. By five P.M., the closing arguments were completed and the judge's instructions were read to the jury. By six P.M. the jury had reached a verdict.

Guilty.

There was only one other time in his life when Jim Casey felt so low. That was when his wife had died. He wasn't surprised at the verdict. All the evidence pointed to him. But he had hoped that somehow, somebody on

19

the jury would believe him. Now his heart was in his stomach, and all the could do was shake his head sadly.

To make matters worse, the judge revoked his bond and ordered him held in the county jail until the sentencing. The sentencing date was set for next Monday at nine o'clock in the morning. This was Friday. Jim Casey would go to prison for a long time. Or hang. Everything he and Boots had worked for would be lost.

"Don't worry. We'll appeal."

He was handcuffed there in the courtroom and marched to the one-cell jail behind the sheriff's office at the end of the converted warehouse on First Street.

Alone in the cell, he sat on one of the two wooden bunks and held his head in his hands. Ever since his wife's death he had talked to her. In their twenty-three years of marriage they'd shared everything. And now, when he had something on his mind, whether it was good or bad, he wanted to share it with her, felt that he was sharing it with her. He mumbled: "I'm in a real jackpot, Boots. Lord, I wish you were here. No, on second thought maybe it's better you're not here. I might be hung. You know I didn't kill anybody. Sure, I had a reason to, but I didn't do it. If nobody else in the whole world believes me, I know you believe me."

Jim Casey was still a moment, then mumbled on, "I feel so helpless. The real killer is around somewhere. I have to find him and prove I'm innocent. How can I do it? How can I do anything locked up like a caged animal?"

More silence, then, "There's only one thing to do, Boots, darlin'. I know you'd agree. If I get killed I won't lose much. Prison or hanging, either way I'll die. No, there's only one thing to do. I've got to bust out of here."

Chapter Three

Dr. Benjamin Woodrow had walked back to his clinic—his five-room clapboard house which he called a clinic—and had started to turn onto the short path to his door when he looked up the street and knew he had another patient. It was the way the rider leaned heavily to the right and hung on to the saddle horn. He was trying to rein the horse up to the hitch rail in front of the house with his left hand and hang on to the saddle horn with the other. He got to the hitch rail before the doctor did, recognized the doctor, and moaned, "Doctor, thank God you're here. I . . . ." The man's face twisted in pain.

Hurrying to his side, Dr. Woodrow said, "Here, let me help you." He got his shoulder under the man, and almost fell when the man's full weight came down on him.

"Sorry, Doc, I . . . cain't hardly . . ." He was on his knees beside the horse, and Dr. Woodrow knew immediately he had an injured right shoulder. Probably a broken collarbone.

"Can you walk at all?"

"I'll shore try, Doc. I got on that horse by myself." A long groan came from him. "Hurts like hell."

"We've got to get you inside the clinic. Wish I had

some help." Looking around, the doctor saw nobody. "See if you can stand and walk."

Face twisted in pain, the man managed to get to his feet and take two steps. But again, he fell to his knees. "Gawd-a-mighty. Gawd it hurts."

Again, the young doctor looked for help. The only human within shouting distance was a woman. A slender woman. She wouldn't be any help.

Squatting, getting a shoulder under the injured man's left arm, Dr. Woodrow said, "Please, sir, try again. We've got to get you inside."

"I'll try, Doc." He got to his feet again, and with the doctor's help took two steps. His knees sagged, but he managed to stay right side up.

"Keep trying, keep trying."

With groans and grunts, the man took two more steps, then sagged again, almost pushing the doctor down.

"Can I help, Doctor? What can I do to help?" The woman had hurried up. She wore a frown, and her pale blue eyes were sympathetic. "He's been hurt, and I don't know where to take hold of him. What can I do, Doctor?"

"Well, uh ..." She was better than no help at all. "Perhaps, if you can get your shoulder under his arm, up high, perhaps I can get in front of him and let him lean his chest on my back." Thank heavens the man was tall.

"All right, let me have his arm." She got under the arm, while the doctor got his back to the man. "Lean on me, sir. Try to keep your feet moving."

It was slow and awkward, with the patient groaning and mumbling, the doctor reaching behind himself and holding him up by his belt. But finally they got him inside, next to the examination table. "Shall we try to lift him up there, Doctor?"

"No. I think, at least for the time being, he's better off on the floor. Would you be so kind as to get a pillow from the bedroom over there and take a blanket off the bed."

"Sure, Doctor."

They got the injured one on his back on the floor, a blanket and a feather pillow under him. "Now I have to get his shirt off and see what kind of injury we have here."

"I'll help." With nimble fingers she started unbuttoning the muslin shirt. Pain had forced the patient's eyes shut, but now he opened them enough to see what was happening.

"You . . . you're a woman. I . . . oh, Lord."

She said, "Don't be embarrassed. I've done this before."

"You have?" Dr. Woodrow took a good look at her now, and was surprised to recognize the so-called daughter of the so-called Dr. Abraham.

Without returning his gaze, she said, "Yes. It's the right shoulder, isn't it? I won't try to move it. Where are your scissors, Doctor?"

"Oh, uh . . ." For a moment he couldn't turn his eyes away from her. "Oh, it's in the top drawer over there."

Within seconds he had the scissors in his hand, and soon he had the shirt cut off. His fingers went over the shoulder and arm, groping, probing. When he persuaded the patient to raise up a few inches, he probed the shoulder blade. The patient inhaled sharply and groaned.

"Is anything fractured?" the young woman asked.

"No. I don't find any fractures. His shoulder is dislocated. That can be extremely painful. I'll have to give him an injection of morphine." Dr. Woodrow stood and went to his instrument cabinet. He wiped a needle-sharp syringe with alcohol, inserted it in a small bottle, and withdrew half a grain of liquid morphine. Kneeling at the patient's side, he swabbed his right arm with alcohol, then quickly injected the liquid. "That should give you some relief within a few minutes, Mr., uh . . .?"

"Delaney. Joseph Delaney. What'd I bust, Doc?"

"You have a dislocated shoulder. How did it happen?"

"Fixin' my roof. Fell off."

"Are you feeling any pain now?"

"No. What're you gonna do?"

"Reset your shoulder. It's a simple procedure. You'll be fine."

Joseph Delaney's face was relaxed. His eyes were half-closed. The young woman stood and watched as the doctor sat on the floor, took off his left shoe, and put the heel of his foot into the patient's right armpit. He took hold of the right arm with both hands and pulled it out along the floor at a right angle to the body. Then he pulled the arm in a half-circle down to the patient's side and at the same time kicked him sharply in the armpit.

The patient grunted, and the woman flinched as the bone snapped back into the socket.

"I know it hurt," Dr. Woodrow said, standing, "but not nearly as badly as it would have without the morphine."

"Is he all right, now, Doctor?"

"Yes. He'll be fine as soon as the morphine wears off."

Joseph Delaney was resting comfortably on the floor. Dr. Woodrow knelt and felt the pulse in his wrist. When he straightened up, he said, "I certainly thank you, Miss, uh, Abraham, isn't it?"

"Yes. I was coming to see you."

"You wanted to see me?"

"Yes. It's about my father. He's a lunger, and I was hoping you could help him."

"He has tuberculosis?"

"Yes. It's getting worse. We came here from Wyoming, hoping this climate would help, but it doesn't seem to help at all."

She was pretty. The doctor couldn't help taking in her curly blond hair, high cheekbones, short, pert nose, full lips, and round, firm chin. He found himself stammering, "Why, uh, I'm afraid I've had no experience with TB, but according to the latest medical journals there still is no cure. I, too, have heard that the dry climate here is of some help."

Frowning, she shook her head. "He'll have to give up his patent medicine business. He can't advertise his own medicine while he's having a coughing fit."

"No, I, uh, I wouldn't think so. Tell me, is he coughing blood?"

"No. That's a good sign, isn't it?"

"I think so. Does he have these seizures often?"

"More and more often. Dr. Woodrow, I want you to know something about my father." Her pale blue eyes were locked onto his, and her face was serious. "My father is not a quack. He was an orderly in the war and he assisted the surgeons many times. Though he never went to medical school, he learned something about medicine and surgical procedures. When we settled in Newhall, in the Territory of Wyoming, there was no doctor for seventy-five miles, and when folks learned that my father knew something of medicine, they came to him."

"Uh-huh." Any thoughts of being sarcastic about a phony doctor were far from his mind now. He wanted to learn more about this young woman. He asked, "Is that

25

where you acquired your experience in aiding the sick and wounded."

"Yes, I helped. My father didn't call himself a doctor then, and he wanted everyone to know that he'd had no formal education in medicine. But he did help some folks. As a matter of fact, he helped a lot of folks. Of course," she was looking down now, "there were folks we couldn't help. A real doctor probably could have."

"I see." He had to clear his throat. "A-hem. There are patients whom no one can help. We just have to do the best we can."

"But apparently there is no help for my father."

"Well, now, I've been advised of a sanitarium some-where near Colorado City where TB patients can live in relative comfort. Though there is no cure, the patients' lives are extended somewhat."

"Oh, there is?" Hope flooded her features and her eyes were brighter. "Do you know any more about it? What's the name of this place? How can we find out about it?"

"I received a folder in the mail advertising the sani-tarium. I'll try to find it. You should understand, how-ever, that you can't always believe the advertisements." For a second he thought of saying the same thing about the patent medicine hawkers, but didn't. Her smile made him glad he didn't.

"Oh, I would like to know more about it. If I had their name and address I would write to them."

"I'll try to find it, but first I think our patient needs some attention."

Joseph Delaney was wide awake now and starting to sit up. "Whew, that was some knockout drop you gave me, Doc." He felt his right shoulder with his left hand. "I reckon ever'thing is back in place."

"Yes, but don't move your shoulder yet. I'll fix a

sling for your arm." Using white cotton cloth, he fash-
ioned a sling for the arm, and advised his patient to
keep the arm and shoulder immobile for a few days.
"When you do move it, do so with a great deal of care.
If you feel any pain, come back."

"I'll do 'er, Doc. Let's see if I can stand up." Taking
the doctor's hand, he pulled himself to his feet. "Good
as new. I shore do thank you. What do I owe you?" He
fumbled in the pockets of his baggy wool pants.
"Uh-oh. I was hurtin' so bad I didn't put my money bag
in my pocket. Can I pay you later?"

"Yes." Dr. Woodrow couldn't help releasing a sigh.
He was used to this. He was also tired of not being paid.

"Now if I can get my shirt on."

"Here, let me help." The young woman held what re-
mained of the muslin shirt while the man got his left
arm in it, then she buttoned the buttons.

"My garsh, you shore are purty."

Ignoring the compliment, she said, "You'll soon learn
to do things with one hand. Can you get on your horse
without help?"

"Yup. He's a gentle ol' pony. I'll, uh, I'll settle with
you next time I come to town, Doc."

"Of course." Silently, he wished the patient would
call him doctor instead of doc.

They were quiet for a moment after Joseph Delaney
left, then Dr. Woodrow said, "I'll try to find that folder
for you." That was when they heard the yelling in the
street.

Someone yelled, "Guilty. He's guilty."

Another man farther away, yelled, "He done it. I
knowed he done it."

More voices came from the street, and the young
woman said, "They must be talking about the murder

27

trial. You testified, didn't you, Doctor. Do you know the man, the defendant?"

"Yes, I know him."

"Do you think he's guilty?"

"Well, I . . ." He didn't know how to answer, but somehow, deep in his guts, he had a hunch that Jim Casey hadn't killed anyone. "I don't know. I just don't know. He doesn't seem to be . . . well, let me find that folder for you."

"Oh, I hope they don't hang an innocent man."

Dr. Woodrow paused, unhappy thoughts going through his mind. "That would be terrible. Just terrible."

"You really believe he's innocent, don't you, Doctor?" Her blue eyes were locked onto his again.

How did she know? How did she read his thoughts? Why was this woman, whom he'd just met, probing his thoughts?

She said, "Is there anything you can do?"

Did she have him flustered! "Why, uh, I, uh know of nothing." He shook his head sadly. "If I knew of anything I could do, believe me, I . . ." He was still shaking his head.

She'd read him like a book. Her voice was soft, understanding. "You'd do it, wouldn't you, Doctor? You'd do anything for a friend, wouldn't you?"

Chapter Four

His only visitor was Levi. The deputy sheriff had taken Levi's gun, an old cap and ball Army Colt, and stood in the open door between the sheriff's office and the cell. Levi had to talk in a low tone, barely above a whisper.

"I'm gonna bust you out of here, Jim. Me and one a the boys are figgerin' out a way."

"No, Levi. I don't want you in trouble with the law." Casey was gripping the cell bars, his face close to Levi's.

"I gotta do somethin'."

"No. Don't do anything."

"You want out, don't you?"

"Sure, but it's my problem. You and the boys keep out of it. Don't get yourselves locked up, too."

"Listen." Levi had a strong urge to glance back at the deputy, but he knew that would make the deputy suspicious. "I've done some lookin', and this old warehouse was built of one-inch lumber. What they done when they built the jail was add some two-inch planks and bolt most of 'em in place. But not all of 'em. There's no way we can get them bars out of the window without tearing out the whole side of the buildin', but . . ."

"Don't do it, Levi. I can try running for it. Maybe when they bring me my supper after dark, I can knock the deputy over and run."

"You can't run fast enough. Listen, some a them planks at the bottom are nailed on. I can bring a crowbar from the rancho, you know, the one we dig post holes with, and pry a couple a them planks loose."

"They'd know you did it, and then you'd be running from the law."

"I run from the law before."

"I suspected that."

"But you was good 'nuff not to say anything. Anyways, what I can do is pry 'em loose so you can kick 'em out from inside. Then I'll get that crowbar back to the ranch right fast."

"Hmm." Casey ran it through his mind. It might work. If Levi could loosen the planks, he might be able to finish the job from inside. And if no pry bar was found and nobody was seen with a pry bar, maybe the sheriff wouldn't suspect he had help.

"Whatta you think, Jim?"

"Maybe . . . but the sheriff will give you a bad time anyway. Maybe what we ought to do is, you get the boards loose, put that crowbar where nobody will find it, then get yourself over to the saloon where a lot of men will see you. That'll give you an alibi. I'll wait until I know you're over there before I try to kick the planks out."

"I'll do 'er. Won't nobody know but you and me. I'll watch for a chance to sneak that crowbar to town. I'll leave a horse for you behind the saloon."

"No. Don't do that. If you leave a horse they'll know I had some help. No, I'll just have to hoof it. I can get away in the dark."

Levi had a question, an important one, but the deputy

interrupted. "I don't know what you two're whisperin' about, but you've whispered long enough. Time for you to haul your ass out of here, old man, and if anything happens I'll come lookin' for you."

Speaking louder, Levi said, "Keep your chin up, Boss." He turned and stomped his high-heeled boots past the deputy without looking at him. In the sheriff's office, beyond the connecting door, he turned and said, "Where's my gun?"

Looking over his shoulder, the deputy said, "Hangin' on the wall. If you could see you'd see it." To Casey, he grumbled, "I should of arrested that skinny old bat in the courtroom. He's lucky he ain't in there with you."

Casey said, "Yeah, yeah."

The more he thought about Levi's plan the more he liked it. Not that it was perfect. Far from it. But he could think of nothing better. Knock over a deputy and run? Hardly. He'd have to knock the deputy out, and that was risky. Hitting a man hard enough to knock him out was taking a chance on killing him. He didn't want to kill anybody. Besides, the deputy was careful. He held a six-gun in his hand with the hammer back every time he opened the cell door, and he always ordered Casey to stand back in the far corner.

Levi's way wouldn't be easy, but it was the only way. First, he'd have to wait until there was nobody at the ranch buildings to see him carry the crowbar away. The bar was a six-foot length of rounded heavy steel with a chisel at one end. It was used to pound out post holes in the rocks. Carrying it on a horse was awkward. When Casey had had to take the bar horseback he'd tied a rope on the chisel end, raised the end up to the horse's shoulder, and wrapped the rope around his saddle horn. That way, once the horse quit boogering at the damned thing, he could drag it.

But Levi wouldn't want to leave drag marks on the ground, so he'd have to carry it across his saddle. His next problem would be getting into town with it without being seen. And after he'd used it he'd have to get it out of town and back to the ranch.

Aw hell, it was hopeless. It would take a lot of luck, and luck was something Jim Casey seemed to be out of.

Levi would try. Casey was sure of that. Now that he'd had more time to think about it he wished he'd talked the old man out of it.

Huh. Casey sat on the iron bunk and recalled the day he'd met the old man. Levi had come riding up to the barn, asking for a job. His horse was well fed on the free grass, but the old man looked like he hadn't had a square meal in a month.

Casey was planning to hire another man, but he wanted a strong man. This drifter looked to be around seventy, skinny, with a long-jawed face covered with wrinkles. When he talked, Casey could see that he had only about half his front teeth. He didn't look capable of picking up a hundred-pound bag of grain. But Casey said, "Get down, mister. When did you eat last?"

"While back. I can work, Mr. Casey. I can keep up with anybody."

"The cook's about to holler 'Chuck.' There are three other men here, and we all eat in the house. Come on in and put your feet under a table."

"I shore appreciate it, Mr. Casey." He held out a leathery hand. "Name's Levi." Casey shook with him.

The hired cowboys were always polite in the house, always wiped their boots and took their hats off before they came in. Casey sat at the head of the table with Mrs. Casey at his right. Meals were eaten quietly. The only conversation was when someone asked someone else to please pass something. Mrs. Carter, middle-aged,

32

fat, and good-natured, kept busy putting platters of roast beef and potatoes on the table. The cowboys, on their way outside, scraped their plates and put them in a big tin dishpan on the stove. They always complimented the cook.

"Mighty good chuck, Miz Carter."

"Shore was good, ma'am."

"Best cobbler I ever threw a lip over."

As the cowboys would say it, the C Bar outfit "fed good."

Outside, Casey tried to think of a way to turn down the old gent's request for a job. But Levi guessed what he was thinking and said, "Even if you don't hire me, Mr. Casey, I'll be tickled to do some work to pay for that meal. Maybe I can chop some wood for the cook, or pump some water, or rake out a corral."

"You don't have to do anything, Levi. I wish I had a job for you, but I'm pretty well filled up now. There are some other ranchers farther south and a few farms that are big enough to hire help."

The screen door slammed and Boots came out, wearing a man's denim clothes and, as always, riding boots. "Where are you from, Levi?" she wore a pleasant expression.

"Texas, ma'am."

"You're a cowboy, I can see that."

"Yes, ma'am. I know cows and cow herds. I know horses, too. I can cowboy with the best of 'em and I can shoe horses, clean corrals, and even shovel hay when I have to."

"Where did you work last?"

The old gent looked down at his boots now. "Last cow outfit I worked for was the Oxbow over in the panhandle country of Texas."

"Let me ask you something, Levi." Boots's eyes were

locked onto the old man's, and Casey knew she wanted a direct and honest answer. That was her way. When she wanted to say something she said it without working around it. "Are you wanted by the law?"

The old gent was wise enough to know he couldn't fool her. He looked up and held her gaze. "No, ma'am, I ain't. I ain't runnin' nor hidin' from nobody, and I don't owe nobody nothin'."

It was Boots who finally looked away. "Can't we find a place for him, Jim?"

"Well, uh . . ." Jim had him figured out now. The man had been in trouble somewhere, but it had been resolved. He'd served his time in jail, maybe. Or something. But Boots liked his face and the way he was so eager to work. And she liked the way he'd answered her questions. Casey liked the way he was willing to do anything that needed doing, instead of making it understood that he hated work that couldn't be done on a horse. Looking at Levi, he said, "How does twenty-five a month and chuck sound?" That was what all the hands started at, and Casey wasn't going to take advantage of this man's desperation.

"Fair 'nuff. I'll start to work right now. What do you want me to do?"

"First thing pick out an empty cot in the bunkhouse and unroll your blankets on it. Put your horse in the corral over there, and we'll turn him out with the remuda tonight."

"Yassir, Mr. Casey."

"Jim. If you're gonna work for me call me Jim."

That was five years ago, and old Levi turned out to be one of the best hands on the outfit. He was especially good with a catch rope, and when they branded calves, he always caught the calves by both hind legs which made it easier for the wrestlers. He roped hard and fast,

Texas style. That is he tied the end of his rope to the saddle horn instead of taking dallies. When he got into a wreck with a big cow and a small horse, he kept calm and got both animals untangled and unhurt. Casey had a hunch old Levi had at some time or other used his skill with a rope to catch cattle he had no business catching, but he kept his hunch to himself.

Now, sitting on a steel cot in a town jail, he mumbled, "Kind of strange, isn't it, Boots. You don't always know who your best friends are gonna turn out to be."

Chapter Five

All he could do was wait. Wait and listen. Saturday night he lay on the bunk wide awake. When Levi came it would be at night. Casey pictured in his mind the lay of the land behind the jail. There were three or four vacant lots, then a few houses, then about five miles of prairie, and then the foothills. The foothills were rocky, with a few tall pines, and brushy with scrub oak in places. The C Bar headquarters was east and south, but the C Bar land surrounded the town on two sides. They ran cattle in the mountains to the west in the summer, and wintered them on the C Bar patented land.

A permanent cow camp, called the Squaw Mountain camp, was established in a homestead on the south end. Two off-breed camps were manned in the mountains during the summer. A man with a wife and two kids was hired to hold down the Squaw Mountain camp. In the off-breed camps, cowboys batched.

Good hideouts for a stranger. But not for Casey. If Sheriff Walt Jackson didn't know about those camps, he'd be sure to find out. They'd be among the first places he'd look. Casey had to find someplace else to hide from the law.

Lying awake, listening for any sound from outside, he tried to think of a hiding place. There were a few prospectors' camps higher in the mountains, and some of them were now unused. No. The sheriff would be sure to search them, too. No buildings of any kind would do.

Let's see, he said to himself, exactly what do I need? He needed a place that wasn't too far away. He needed a horse and he needed some chuck. If he was going to do any detective work, try to find out who did kill that preacher, he'd have to stay somewhere near town. And he wished he could keep an eye on his ranch and live-stock, but that was hopeless. He'd have to depend on his hired help.

Thinking of that brought a bitter bile to his throat. They wouldn't stay. He couldn't blame them. With him dead or in prison, there'd be nobody to pay them. Levi would be there, but he couldn't watch everything. Hell, he could keep an eye on only a small part of the ranch, the headquarters buildings.

Casey put an arm over his eyes and groaned. With him in prison and no hired help, the squatters and rus-tlers would steal everything but the land and buildings. And the state and county would take that for back taxes. Lord, he groaned, everything he and Boots had worked for would be gone.

Sheriff Jackson had been out of the office, but now he was back. Soon the deputy would take over and the sheriff would go home. Jackson kept a canvas folding cot in his office so he could catch a few winks and keep his office open at the same time. When there was no prisoner in the jail, they locked the office at night and slept in their own beds. Now that they had a prisoner, one of them had to be in the office or nearby at all times.

Casey wondered if Levi knew of their routine.

Somewhere around ten o'clock, the deputy came in and the sheriff went home. Casey could barely hear their voices through the closed door. When he could no longer hear them, he guessed that the sheriff had left. Under his breath Casey said, "Wait a couple more hours, Levi."

But Levi didn't come at all that night.

Sunday Casey walked from one end of the small cell to the other. About a hundred times. He wished he had some tobacco. He'd quit smoking four years ago, but now if he had the makings he'd roll himself a cigarette. Smoking was bad for the health, they said. Cigarettes were coffin nails. Huh! His health was the last thing Casey had to worry about now.

For supper he had the usual fried spuds and tough beef from the Rockledge Cafe. The coffee was only lukewarm by the time the deputy brought it over. "Stand back," the deputy warned. "Get over there in that corner." Sheriff Jackson unlocked the cell door, and he, too, had a six-gun in his hand as the deputy carefully placed the plate and cup on the plank floor.

While he was in the cell, the deputy took a careful look around at the floor and the walls for any sign of chiseling. He tested the window bars and found them still solid.

What did they think he'd cut the floor and walls with, Casey asked himself after they left. They'd taken his pocket knife. Did they think he'd chew his way out like a big rat?

Both the sheriff and his deputy came back to get the empty plate and the slop bucket. The deputy growled, "Keep quiet and we'll get along fine."

Now why did he say that? Casey hadn't raised a ruckus yet. But maybe some prisoners did. A drunk's yelling could get on the deputy's nerves. It wouldn't take much to get on the deputy's nerves. That, no doubt, is why they kept the connecting door shut.

Dark was a long time coming on an August night. It was hot in the cell. Casey kept his shirt off most of the time. Sweat burned his eyes and made his armpits itch.

He paced the cell some more. He took hold of the window bars and pulled himself up to where he could look outside. It was just as he'd remembered, weed-grown vacant lots and shacks with tin roofs a few town blocks away. First Street ran in front of the converted warehouse, but it was out of Casey's sight. A half-block down the street was one of the two saloons. Across the street was the Farmer's State Bank and next to that was the Front Range Hotel. Farther down First Street was a blacksmith shop, and across from the blacksmith shop was the Howell Mercantile.

Two blocks east on a cross street was Dr. Woodrow's five-room clapboard house and clinic. What he called a clinic.

The mercantile was the first business in Rockledge. Tudor Howell had hauled his merchandise from Denver to stock a small room and sell groceries, tobacco, and rifle ammunition to the prospectors who roamed the mountains over west. Jim and Boots Casey appreciated the store and bought most of their supplies there. The homesteaders, when they began moving in, were also customers. Howell enlarged the room. A year later he enlarged it again and reserved a corner for a druggist.

Drummers came to town in their one-horse buggies to sell to the store and to the homesteaders. Some of them went from farm to farm, selling everything from needles and thread to patent medicine. They needed a place to spend their nights, and a single-story hotel was built.

The Prospectors Saloon opened for business with a plank bar and card tables. Two brothers from Denver built a barrel factory that employed eight men. Business was good enough that a man named Schultz opened the Gold Dust Saloon, this one with a mahogany bar, pictures on the wall, spittoons, a privy for the ladies, and a billiard table. The ladies' privy wasn't used. No respectable woman would inhabit a saloon, and Sheriff Jackson kept the prostitutes out of town.

The Farmers Bank was a brick building with thick pine doors and strong locks. A safe was brought by wagon from Denver. Dr. Woodrow had come to town from somewhere back east, and he'd no more than hung out his shingle than he had all the patients he could take care of. When Colorado joined the Union as a full-fledged state a few years ago, the General Assembly divided one big county into two small ones, and made Rockledge a county seat. It was the only town in the new county.

But now most of the prospectors had given up on the mountains straight west, and were having better luck farther north around the town of Black Hawk. And at least half the farmers had quit trying to grow crops in Eastern Colorado's dry climate and were moving back to Kansas and Missouri. Were it not for the C Bar Ranch, Oak County couldn't collect enough taxes to hire a sheriff, much less a deputy.

"Shit," Jim Casey said to himself as he paced the jail floor. "Excuse me, Boots. I know you don't like that kind of language. But it just frosts my ass to think about how we're paying most of the taxes in this damned

40

county and folks around here treat me like I was Simon Legree. That damned preacher had folks thinking I was Satan himself. And the damned stupid farmers believed everything he said."

Casey flopped down on the bunk and put an arm over his eyes.

It was quiet. Daylight slowly faded. When Casey opened his eyes again, it was dark. There was no lamp in the cell. Too many drunks had been locked up in it, and some of them were crazy enough to start a fire. Under the connecting door, a sliver of light showed. Soon the deputy would come to relieve the sheriff. Casey sat up, listening. Levi would have to come tonight or Monday night. He was to be sentenced on Monday. If he was condemned to hang, they wouldn't wait long to haul him down to Canon City and the state prison. That was where they did their hanging nowadays. Most of the time.

He'd be handcuffed and hobbled and made to walk with short steps to a wagon, then hauled east to the railroad. While other railroad passengers gawked he'd be transported to Pueblo, then loaded on a wagon again for the last leg of the trip to Canon City.

Most folks would want him hung right here to save time and money, but that wasn't the way it was supposed to be done. Now that Colorado was divided into state judicial districts and had its own prison, there was a right way and a wrong way. The judges and lawyers wanted everything done legally.

They didn't always get their way.

There'd been times when the citizens didn't agree with the law and the courts, and mobs had busted open jails and hung the convicted. In fact, there were times when they didn't wait for a conviction.

Who knows what's gonna happen, Casey mumbled to himself.

He guessed it was 11:30 or 12 o'clock when he heard a noise from outside.

Chapter Six

Jim Casey heard the noise again. It was at the side of the building, behind the jail. Had to be Levi. At first, it was a pounding. Levi had to pound the end of a plank with the chisel end of the crowbar to get the bar behind it. Now it was a prying sound. Nails creaked.

Casey wondered if the deputy was asleep on the cot. Those damned nails didn't come loose easily. Nails, hell. Long spikes. They creaked, and anybody who'd ever pried nails loose would recognize the sound.

Yanking the blankets off both bunks, Casey rolled them up and shoved them against the wall, hoping to muffle the sound. Be quiet, Levi, he muttered under his breath. He knew Levi couldn't be quiet. There was no way to pry those planks loose without making a noise.

Half-expecting to see the connecting door yanked open and the deputy standing in it with a gun in his hand, Casey breathed shallowly as the prying continued. At least Levi was making progress. Keep it up, Levi, but be as quiet as you can.

The sound ceased for a moment. Casey guessed that one plank was loose. The planks were a foot wide. Levi had to pry two more loose. The prying began again.

All Casey could do was hope. Keeping an eye on the

connecting door, he hoped, listened, and waited. Once the bottom plank was loose it would be easy to get the end of the crowbar behind the next one. Spikes creaked. Then it was quiet again.

Did Levi see or hear somebody coming? Was he flat on the ground in the weeds staying out of sight, waiting for somebody to go on past? It seemed like an hour but probably was only five minutes before the prying continued.

Good thing that crowbar was six feet long. It took that much leverage to pry those spikes out. Just get them halfway out, Levi, and I can kick the boards loose.

A pause outside, then more prying. Spikes creaked. Good thing that side of the warehouse was backed by vacant ground. Still, the deputy might hear it. Or somebody else might hear it and warn the deputy. Casey's heart was beating too fast. Any second the deputy could get suspicious and come running. He'd come with a six-gun in one hand and a lamp in the other. Levi wouldn't know the deputy was in the cell and he'd keep working.

Finally, the noise ceased again. Casey listened. When he heard no more creaking spikes, he guessed that Levi had three or four planks pried loose and had left.

What Casey had to do now was sit on the floor and kick the one-inch boards off from the inside, then kick the planks until the ends were opened enough for him to squeeze out. But not yet. Give Levi time to hide the crowbar somewhere outside town and get back to the saloon. Wait until Levi was where he'd be seen.

Again, Casey wished he had the makings of a cigarette. Even if cigarettes did make his throat raw. Even if he did wake up coughing every morning. Anything would be better than just sitting here in the dark and doing nothing. He wanted to get out of here, get started.

Started where?

All right, Jim Casey, he said to himself, think. You've been all over this end of the county and those mountains up there. You've chased cattle every place cattle could go, and you know the country better than anybody else. Think. He worried about it, trying to remember every hard-to-find spot he'd ever seen. Then it came to him.

A box canyon. Just a pocket at the bottom of a high ridge. Almost straight west, about six miles. One end of the short canyon and its sides were straight up. The open end faced east. Casey and Levi had chased an old longhorn bull in there a few years ago, and had looked for more cattle in there since then. It was hard to find because of the buck brush that grew so thick across the open end. A man on foot had to bend low and push his way through the brush. A man on horseback had a hell of a time. In fact, the first time they'd been in there, Levi had stayed outside and held Casey's horse while Casey crawled through the brush on his hands and knees just to see what was on the other side.

The old bull had had himself a private paradise. There was about half an acre of good green grass in there, and a spring that seeped out of the foot of the south side. It spread shallow water over half the open ground before seeping back into the ground under the brush.

That's where Casey would go. When the time came.

He waited for what he guessed was two hours before he started. There'd been no sound from outside nor from inside for that long. The deputy was asleep on the cot, or fighting to stay awake.

Casey sat on the floor, pulled his boots off, put the wadded blankets next to the wall and kicked the bottom with one foot. Nothing happened. Kicked again.

Dammit, this wasn't going to be easy. And though his sock feet made little noise, it wasn't going to be perfectly quiet. What was worse, kicking with his bare heels seemed to be getting nowhere. It would be easier with his boots on, but his boots would be too noisy. He kicked again, harder, so hard it hurt his heels. Again and again, ignoring the pain. A board came loose. Casey stopped, listened. Nothing.

Rewadding the blankets, he put them against the board and again kicked with both feet. The blankets partially muffled the noise, but anybody listening would hear it. He wished a wagon would go by outside with rattling trace chains and squeaky wheels. He wished it weren't so damned quiet in the town. Kicked again. Now two boards were loose. He could put a hand outside. Groping with his fingers, he discovered that the spikes which had held the planks were completely free of the building, but were sticking through the planks. Well, he could bend the planks a little bit.

After listening a moment, he resumed his kicking until the nails in the one-inch boards came free and he could push the boards out of his way.

No use stopping now. If the deputy came in to investigate the noise it would all be over. He wished he had that crowbar inside. But no, the deputy and the sheriff would know he'd had help. He had to make them believe he'd done it all himself. He kicked. He pushed with his hands.

Sweet, fresh air came in from outside, cooling the temperature in the cell. Working feverishly, Casey pushed the boards and planks far enough away from the building that he hoped he could crawl out.

Now's the time to try it, he said under his breath.

First, he shoved his boots out through the opening, then, on his belly, he slithered like a snake and got his head outside. The night was black. Good. But he couldn't get his shoulders through. He pulled his head back inside, sat on the floor, and pushed on the planks with his feet. They moved. Again, he lay on his belly and crawled. This time he got his shoulders outside, but a nail tore his shirt and cut a shallow gash in his left shoulder.

Grabbing grass and digging his fingers into the ground, he pulled himself through the opening. A spike snagged his belt, but he was able to reach back with one hand and unsnag it.

Then he was out.

A dog barked somewhere. Otherwise the town was quiet. The cool night air smelled and tasted delicious, and Casey breathed deeply. He pulled his boots on and walked across a weed-grown lot in the dark, heading west. He stumbled, falling into a shallow hole somebody had dug for something or other. Damned farmers were always tearing up the ground. Stepping out of the hole, he went on. He was a hundred yards behind one of the saloons now, and he could see a dim light in a window. Across a vacant lot, a lamp lit up a cabin window. All the other houses were dark. Another dog barked.

No use trying to sneak out of town. If he was seen in the dark, maybe he wouldn't be recognized. Stand up straight and walk like a man who's going home. If he tried to be sneaky, anyone who saw him would be suspicious.

Walking was never Casey's favorite pastime, but it felt so good to be out of that jail that he enjoyed walking. Looking at the sky, he saw no moon. He didn't know what time it was or how long until daylight. Staying away from any street or road where he might be seen, he walked across vacant land until he was out of town.

He knew where he wanted to go, and instincts told him he was going in the right direction. All he had to do was stay out of sight of anything human until he got there.

Now that he was out of town he walked faster, broke into a trot at times. It would be best if he got close to the canyon before daylight. A rattlesnake buzzed its warning off to his right. Goddam. He'd never worried about snakes when he was horseback. Horses nearly always survived snakebites. But a man on foot would be a fool not to worry about rattlers. Stepping wide, he walked on. Then a new worry entered his mind. He had to have chuck, a skillet, matches, blankets, a horse. He couldn't just walk into the Howell Mercantile and buy what he needed. Besides, he had no money. The sheriff had emptied his pockets. Somebody would have to fetch that stuff for him. Levi would do it.

But would Levi figure out where he was?

Chapter Seven

The poker game went on most of the night. Levi
wasn't trying to win, but he couldn't afford to lose
much either. Especially when he didn't know where his
next paycheck was coming from. Jim had been paying
his help with drafts on the Farmers State Bank, but now
there would be no paychecks. Not as long as Jim was
wanted by the law. Levi played a conservative game.
His only reason for being in the game was to be sure he
was seen. He wasn't nervous. He'd lived through more
than his share of suspense. But he couldn't concentrate
on the game either, couldn't help wondering whether
Jim had made it outside and was on his way
somewhere—afoot. He wished he'd had a chance to ask
Jim where he was planning to hide. If that deputy had
given him ten seconds more, he'd have asked.

At 3:10 A.M. by the clock on the wall, he drew two
jacks and had a jack in the hole. It looked like a win-
ning hand. But he had only a dollar and a half in the
pot, and if he won the pot he'd have to stay longer and
give the other three players a chance to win it back. He
folded, scooted back his chair, and allowed, "Weel, better get back to the rancho. Got no boss, but somebody's
got to stick around and keep the thieves away."

"You gonna work for nothing, Levi?"

"Reckon so. For a while anyway."

He figured he had about two more hours of darkness when he tightened the cinch on his horse and rode out of town. At the edge of town, in a narrow weed-filled gulley, he groped the ground for the crowbar, laid it across the fork of his saddle, mounted, and rode on. The movements of the horse caused the crowbar to continually slide so it was out of balance across the saddle. Levi had to hang on to it with one hand, and the damned thing was heavy. At the C Bar barn, he put the tool back exactly where it had been, unsaddled his horse and turned him out. Only one man was asleep in the bunkhouse. The others were batching in the cowcamps, keeping C Bar cattle somewhere this side of the divide, roping and branding cattle that had been missed in the roundups, and doctoring sick cattle the best way they could. Levi was going to have to ride up to the camps and deliver the news: the boss was either going to hang or spend a long time in prison. Nobody else had authority to sign paychecks.

The one man in the bunkhouse raised up on his bed, struck a match, and lit a lamp on a small, badly scarred table next to his bed. He also lit a cigarette that he'd rolled the night before.

"Been tomcattin', Levi? Anything new?"

"Naw." Levi sat on his own bunk and pulled off his boots. "Jim's s'posed to be sentenced this afternoon. Most folks think the judge won't have 'im hung, but he'll spend maybe the rest of his life in that goddam prison down to Canon City."

"It's a cryin' shame. Jim didn't kill nobody."

"No, but the goddam jury was full of goddam farmers

that hate cowmen, and that goddam holy water woman lied, and ever' damn thing went wrong."

"Whatta you gonna do, Levi?"

"I'm gonna stick around. I know Jim didn't kill that goddam holy roller 'cause I was with 'im when the son of a bitch was shot. I'm no detective, but I'm gonna keep my ears and eyes open, and maybe somethin' will turn up."

"Can I help?"

"I don't know how. Hell, I don't know what to do myself, except listen and watch."

"I reckon I'll haul my freight out of here, then. Maybe I'll give it a couple more days. If nothin' happens there ain't no use hangin' around."

"I don't blame you." Lying back on his bunk, Levi settled his head on his pillow and muttered, "Ever'thing's gone to hell."

Shortly after daylight the word was spreading. Jim Casey had busted out of jail. The first question everyone asked was: How?

"Pushed the goddam boards loose with his feet," the deputy said. "Goddam it, I knew that jail wouldn't hold nobody. Sat on the floor, muffled the noise with some blankets, and pushed the goddam boards loose and crawled out."

"Whatta you gonna do about it?"

"Hunt for 'im, for Chrissake. Run 'im down. Startin' right now."

"Did he have a horse?"

"Shore, he had a horse. You don't think he took off on foot, do you? He either stole a horse or somebody gave him one."

"Who'd a gave 'im one? That old fart, that Levi?"

"Who else?"

Levi was expecting them. Sheriff Waltham Jackson, the piss-headed deputy, and five townsmen rode up to the ranch house on winded horses, and the sheriff got down and pounded on the door. From the barn, Levi watched as Mrs. Carter opened the door, and he heard the sheriff say:

"I think you know why we're here, Miz Carter. We're gonna search the place."

Heard Mrs. Carter's surprised voice, "Why? What happened?"

"I got a suspicion you know, but in case you don't, your boss broke out of jail last night."

"Oh my."

"Of course you haven't seen him? And you don't know anything about it?"

"Why no."

"Well, we're gonna search the place. Come on in, men."

Seven men swarmed through the house, even looked under the house, then came out to the barn. Levi stepped out to meet them. Sheriff Jackson stopped in front of the old gent and said, "Of course you wouldn't know anything about your boss's escape?"

"He escaped?" Levi was doing the best acting job he could. "When?"

"Last night. Of course you wouldn't have anything to do with it?"

"Last night? How'd he do it? Anybody get shot?"

"I've got a suspicion you know how. Where was you last night?"

"In town. Drinkin'. Jawin'. Got in a poker game at the Gold Dust."

"When did you leave the Gold Dust?"

"Dunno. Don't pack no watch. I'd reckon 'bout two o'clock. When did he bust out?"

"Could have been about two o'clock. Of course you came straight back here?"

"Yeah."

"Who else is here?"

"Another cowpuncher."

"Where is he?"

"Wranglin' the horses. We've got work to do."

"Who's gonna pay you?"

With a shrug, Levi answered, "Jim will after you use your head and figure out who killed that preacher."

"You'd get word to him, is that it?"

"How can I do that if I don't know where he is?" Looking at the rising sun a moment, Levi added, "He'll know about it. Read about it in the newspapers, maybe."

"He's had a fair trial and he's been convicted. Now he's an outlaw on the dodge. We'll find him. If he headed for Denver, we'll find him, what with telegraphs and a big city police department and all."

Levi only shrugged.

"We're gonna search the place. Don't you go nowhere. I'm gonna have another talk with you."

"If that's the way you wanta spend your time, have at it. Me, I'm goin' to the house and see if Mrs. Carter's got the coffee on."

As he walked to the house, Levi realized he'd made a mistake by not staying in the Gold Dust until daylight, until the jail break had been discovered. He'd wanted to get the crowbar back to the barn before daylight, but then he'd had it well hidden and he could have done that another night. He felt some better, however, knowing that while the sheriff and his deputy were searching the C Bar headquarters, Jim Casey had more time to make his way to a hiding place.

Let them search. Let them spend all day searching.

It was afternoon when the sheriff gave up. "He could be anywhere," he said, exasperated. "There's just too damn many places to hide."

"His saddle's here," a bearded townsman said. Levi recognized him as the gent who owned a harness shop in town. "I know his saddle. Fixed a busted stirrup leather once. His brand is burned on the top skirt."

"He could have used another saddle. He could have stole a horse and saddle from one of the pens in town."

With a shrug, the harness maker said, "Could have. But if he'd taken a horse from here he'd of used his own saddle."

"Well, like I said, he could be anywhere. He could be hiding behind something and watching us right now. There's just too damn many places to hide." Sheriff Jackson turned hard eyes to Levi. "You. You're coming to town with us. And I'll take that hogleg you're packing. We're gonna lock you up on suspicion 'till we figure out exactly when Jim Casey busted out and where you were at the time."

Being behind bars was nothing new to Levi. He'd been locked up before, although not for over five years now. Hearing a wood drill outside, he knew they were replacing the loose planks. This time they'd use lag screws. Big ones. Ones that couldn't be kicked loose. Good. While they were doing that they'd tromp down any sign he'd left out there. Now they for sure had no evidence against him. With any luck at all he wouldn't be in here long. Still, being in a cage brought back that old cramped, helpless, hopeless, empty-hearted feeling. Just looking at the bars made him uncomfortable. He'd

54

thought he was through being an outlaw, being locked up.

But what worried him most was the predicament his boss was in. Afoot, no chuck, no gun, no blankets, no nothing.

Chapter Eight

Six miles wasn't a long walk for most men, but for a cowman who seldom walked any farther than from the house to the corral, it was tiring as hell. And Casey's riding boots weren't made for walking. At the first sign of dawn he was at the foot of a rocky ridge, crossing the arroyos made by thousands of years of rain and snow runoff. Before he climbed out of an arroyo, he poked his head above the rim and studied his back trail. He saw nobody. They'd discovered his escape by now, but their first stop would be the C Bar headquarters, and when they didn't find him there they'd search the cow camps. Sheriff Waltham Jackson would also have someone, probably the deputy, riding the country between the headquarters and the railroad, thinking he might have made his way to Jack's Corners and got on a train somehow. There was no railroad at Rockledge, but there was a telegraph. The sheriff would send a message to the police in Denver, asking them to be on the lookout for him.

A guilty man would hightail it out of the country. Lose himself somewhere else. A man who hoped to be proved innocent would hide out nearby. Jackson was convinced Casey was guilty. When he failed to find him in the cow camps, maybe he'd figured he'd left the country, and would quit looking.

Maybe. Maybe not.

Climbing hand over hand out of a deep gully, Casey knew he was only a mile or so now from the hidden pocket of a canyon at the bottom of the ridge. He walked, cursed his sore feet, and hobbled on. By sunup he came to the scrub oaks that hid the pocket. He dropped to his hands and knees and crawled, ducking his head to keep the brush from scratching his face. His hat was hanging from a peg in the sheriff's office, and he missed it. He didn't feel right at all outdoors without a hat.

A heavy dew covered the grass and brush, and by the time he got out of the oaks he was thoroughly wet.

Wet and cold.

Shivering in the early morning, he walked across the pocket, noticing with satisfaction that the spring was still soaking one side of it. When he looked up at the granite walls, though, he wished the sun were high enough to send some warmth his way. He sat on a small boulder and hugged his knees. His stomach growled. "Shut up," he mumbled.

There was no sign of any animal bigger than a coyote ever having been here. The cow pies, or in this case bull pies, had been washed away years ago. The grass, mostly timothy, was knee high and hadn't been grazed on.

The sun was far enough above the horizon now that it was shining in Casey's face. Happy that the mouth of the pocket faced east, he tilted his head back and soaked up the warmth. It stopped his shivering. Now what he needed was something to eat.

Sitting there, Casey wished for two things: he wished old Levi would bring him some chuck, blankets, and matches. And a horse. He also wished he wouldn't. Not for a couple of days. Not until the sheriff and whatever posse he could gather had searched the cow camps and miners' camps, and the whole damned county. A couple of days? Better make that three or four days. Getting a horse through the brush would leave sign that a sharp-eyed lawman or posseman could see. Wait, Levi, Casey said under his breath. I won't starve.

Or would he? He had water, and he wouldn't die of dehydration. But there was a limit to how long a man could go without eating.

The boy was six, and he opened his mouth readily when Dr. Woodrow asked him to. Sitting on the end of the examination table, he said, "Ahh," at the doctor's request.

"There's some inflammation of the lymphoid tissue," the doctor told the boy's mother.

"What's that?" She was plain, stringy slender with a thin, homely face.

"Tonsillitis. I can swab it with tincture of opium, but that will help only temporarily. I recommend that you take him to a hospital in Denver and have the tissue removed."

"To a hospital? In Denver? None of us has ever been in a hospital. Cain't you do it?"

"Yes, in an emergency I can do it, but he should be hospitalized for a few days, and the hospitals have better equipment."

"Won't that cost a lot of money?"

"It . . ." How to answer? "It will cost, yes."

"We ain't got no money."

"Uh, Mrs. Doty, there are organizations that help the indigent."

"I ain't even got the money to pay you."

He expected that when he saw her come in. "I will waive my office fee in this case."

"That's right nice of you. Now I have to figger a way to get 'im to Denver."

"I hope you can find a way, Mrs. Doty. His throat is very sore now and it will get worse. If it's absolutely necessary, I'll perform a tonsillectomy here. Meanwhile, it is painful for him to swallow food, so give him all the milk he can drink. Do you have a cow?"

"Yeah, that's about all we got left. Sold our land to that land grabber, that Jim Casey, the one that broke out of jail." The woman was bitter. "Sold it for half of what it's worth."

"What?" Dr. Woodrow paused with a bottle of opium in his hand. "Mr. Casey broke out of jail?"

"Didn't you hear? Ever'body else knows about it. Kicked some boards loose and crawled outta that sorry excuse for a jail." Her voice was pure venom. "I hope they ketch 'im and hang 'im."

"What did he ever do to you? Bought your land, you said?"

"Yeah. Seventy-five cents an acre. Told us we have to get out before winter. My Joe, he had to take a job at the barrel factory, stedda farmin' our own land like we wanted to."

Dr. Woodrow took his meals at the Rockledge Cafe now and then when he just had to have a respite from his own cooking. His pantry was well stocked. Instead of cash, some of his patients paid him with more eggs and meat than he could keep fresh, and his root cellar held more potatoes, carrots, turnips, and cabbages than he could use. His backyard was piled high with firewood, and he had five-gallon cans of coal oil for his lamps.

The cafe was not a good place for a doctor. He'd no more than sit down than someone would come up and complain about an illness of some kind. Or someone else's illness. "My woman's got them godawful cramps and the only way I can keep 'er from gettin' 'em is to keep 'er knocked up all the time." How many times had he heard that?

And the wrinkled old woman who waited on him, she was always complaining about her feet killing her, and asking if there was anything he could do about it.

The town needed another doctor. Or a nurse. Even that phony Dr. Abraham could take some of the work load off. But no other doctor would come here to Poverty Pockets, Colorado.

Dr. Woodrow took off his white coat, put on his homburg hat, and walked down the dirt path to First Street. when he saw that whining, belittling Mrs. Agnes Mooreman coming toward him he wished he'd taken a different route.

"Oh, doctor, I was just coming to see you, I've got this awful pain in my stomach, and it just won't go away, and I was hoping you could do something, and it keeps me up most of the night, and if I don't get some sleep purty soon I think I'll just die, and now that the Reverend Weems ain't here to pray over me I'll have to pass on without the proper service."

"I was just going to the cafe to get something to eat, Mrs. Mooreman. I'll be back within the hour."

"Can't you eat later, I hurt something awful and it's been hurting for a long time and it's getting worser and worser and I need some medicine right now and I tried that Chief Red Hawk's Elixer and it didn't do any good and I asked Mr. Samuels over to the store to fix me

60

something and he said he didn't know of anything and I'd have to get a note from you."

"I have a comfortable chair in my waiting room, Mrs. Mooreman, and the latest newspaper from Denver."

"Humph. A body could just up and die in this town and nobody would care now that the Reverend Weems is gone."

"I'll be back within the hour. I promise."

"Humph." But Mrs. Agnes Mooreman turned and walked toward the doctor's clinic-home.

He sat at a table for four in the Rockledge Cafe, head down, hoping no one would notice him. No such luck. He felt, rather than saw, a woman's shape beside him. Trying to ignore her, he studied the menu, which didn't take long. He had his choice between pork sausage and gravy with baking powder biscuits or boiled beef and turnips.

"Dr. Woodrow, can I ask you somethin'?" She was plain, with graying hair pulled back and tied with ribbon. He felt like groaning, but he kept his disappointment to himself. "Why, uh, yes." He stood because he was taught from childhood to stand when approached by a lady.

"My little girl's nose is always runnin', and snot runs down her upper lip, and she's always lickin' it off. I keep tellin' her not to do that 'cause it'll make her sick, but she does it anyway. Will it make her sick, Doctor?"

"Mrs., uh, ma'am, is the, uh, discharge a clear color?"

"It's kinda yellowish. Does that mean anything?"

"You should bring your child to the clinic and let me examine her. She could have an infection in the sinus cavity."

"Will that cost much?"

He wanted to sit. He wanted to be rid of her. He

wanted anything but to stand here and answer questions from this woman. He was about to excuse himself and go back to his clinic-home without eating when help arrived.

She was smiling. She was cheerful. She was pretty. "Hello, Dr. Woodrow. How nice to see you again." Somehow she got between him and the woman, did it without being rude, did it in such a way that the woman said simply, "Thenkyew, Doctor," and left.

"Why, Miss Abraham, it's nice to see you, too." Boy, was it ever. She'd never know how nice. Or would she? Yes, come to think of it, he was sure she knew. "Won't you join me?"

"I'd be happy to."

He hurried around the table and pulled out a chair for her. She was wearing a starched yellow dress with a ruffle at the throat. She was a breath of fresh air.

"I have news, Doctor. My father sold out. He sold his team and wagon and his supply of elixer. A gentleman we met in Wyoming tried to buy him out, but at the time my father wasn't interested in selling. Thanks to the modern telegraph, my father was able to contact him, and the sale was finalized this morning."

"Why, that's, uh, I hope good news, Miss Abraham."

"Definitely good news. My father is going down to Manitou Springs where he'll stay in one of the sanitariums."

"What will you do, Miss Abraham?"

"Well." She bit her lower lip, then quickly forced a smile. "Get a job. Find a place to live. I'm told that Mrs. Spencer's boarding house isn't bad."

"Not that it's any of my business, but I'm curious. What kind of work will you look for?"

Again, she bit her lip, and again she quickly smiled. "Oh, I can do lots of things."

Dr. Woodrow made a sudden decision. "Would you care to work for me?" And just as suddenly he wished he hadn't. "Oh, uh, I should not have said that. Cash for a salary is scarce. Please ignore that question."

She put her chin in her hands and looked with pale blue eyes across the table at him. "I know what you mean. My father had the same problem in Wyoming." Then she smiled. "But we didn't go hungry or cold."

"No, there's that." He had to smile with her. "If you would accept eggs and meat and vegetables and firewood, I could pay you very well." He added quickly, "I'm joking, of course."

Her smile turned into a chuckle. "Who knows, perhaps Mrs. Spencer would be more than happy to accept that in lieu of cash."

Just the thought of it brought a chuckle from him. And he realized that this was his first chuckle in a long time.

Chapter Nine

Attorney Amos P. Sharp had a proposition. But first, he looked back at the deputy standing in the connecting doorway and said in a stern voice, "This gentleman is my client, and we are entitled to some privacy."

"Yeah, well, don't stay more'n a few minutes. I got some ridin' to do."

"Am I your client?" Levi asked after the deputy left. He leaned a shoulder against the bars in the one-cell jail.

"Yes, and I'll tell you why. First, I can get you out of here. Sheriff Jackson admitted he has no real evidence against you, and you haven't been charged with a crime. Second, Mr. Casey owes me money. He paid most of my fee in advance, but not all of it. Second . . ."

"I can guess," Levi said, gripping the bars. "What if I was to tell you I don't know where he is?"

"I'm gambling that you do. And anything you tell me will go no further. As my client, whatever transpires between you and me is privileged."

Levi started to explain that he really didn't know where Jim Casey was, but he changed his mind. Instead, he asked, "What can I do about it?"

"I can make out a check on the Farmers State Bank,

and you can get Mr. Casey to sign it. I'll predate the check so it will look as though it was issued before Mr. Casey's bond was revoked and he was incarcerated."

With a bobbing of his Adam's apple, Levi said simply, "All right."

"Fine. Now, as soon as the sheriff gets back from lunch you'll be free. But for heaven's sake, don't let anyone see you when you contact Mr. Casey."

Not until an hour later, when he was standing with his thumbs hooked inside his gun belt in Amos P. Sharp's room at the Front Range Hotel, did Levi admit that he would have to hunt for his employer.

"Oh my." The lawyer sat on the edge of the bed and stared at the bare wooden floor. "I would have bet that you knew right where to find him."

"Well, don't worry about it. I'll find him. It might take a few days, but I know the country around here and I know Jim, and I'll find 'im."

"Very well." Amos P. Sharp stood and went to the scarred dresser. It, one chair, and the bed were the only furniture in the room. The top drawer was stubborn, and he had to yank on it twice to get it open. He took out a check. "Please explain to Mr. Casey that I have added my fee for filing an appeal, and tell him that I am almost certain that the appellate court will grant him a new trial. I will argue that my motion for a change of venue should have been granted, and that my client had no chance for a fair trial in this county."

"I'll tell 'im."

"It will take time. And money."

"Shore."

"I have also added my fee for representing you."

"Yup."

"I am maintaining this room here in the hotel as a sort of office away from my office, but I will be going back to Denver later today. However, I will return in a few days. You can find me here."

"Yup."

His eyes picked out the four men as soon as he stepped inside the Gold Dust Saloon. They were sitting at a table near the back wall, taking turns pouring whiskey from a quart bottle into shot glasses. They were new in town and they were hardcases. Levi had them cataloged at first glance. It was the way they carried their guns, low, with shell belts stuffed with .44-40 cartridges. And their eyes, shifty, wary, taking him in as he stepped through the open door. Wide-brim hats, trail-dusty clothes, clothes that had been slept in. Cowboys, but not honest ones. Levi was sure of that.

He ordered a beer from a wide-shouldered bartender in a dirty white shirt, and turned his back to the four. While he sipped his beer he tried to figure out a plan. If that lawyer thought he knew where Jim Casey was hiding, then the sheriff had the same thoughts. The sheriff and everybody else.

Unless Jim made it to one of the cow camps. He was hungry but he wouldn't be so dumb as to go to one of the cow camps. In fact, while Levi stood at the bar, he heard, then saw, the sheriff, his deputy, and three other men ride past, going west. Though he got only a quick look at them as they went past the saloon door, he saw that they were armed with six-guns and rifles. They were hunting Jim, and their first stops would be the cow camps.

So where was Jim hiding? And when would the sheriff quit riding and hunting?

The four hardcases were talking louder. The whiskey was unhinging their jaws. One of them laughed, a high-pitched whinney.

Dammit, Levi thought, standing at the bar, Jim's got to be up there in the high country, and it gets cold up there at night. Jim's not only hungry, he's cold.

"Goddam," one of the four said in a loud voice, "I feel like letting off some steam like one a them railroad engines."

Another said, "Wonder if there's anything to do for fun in this pisswater town."

"Hey, barkeep, is there a whorehouse around here?"

"Naw," the husky bartender said.

Ignoring them, Levi tried to figure out what to do. He couldn't go looking for his employer for a few days, that was certain. Jim would be uncomfortable, but hell, he was one of the first to settle in this country, and he'd been cold and hungry before. He'd live.

"Well, how the hell does a feller get his socks warshed? Is there any women around here?"

"Naw."

"Was that the shurff that went by?"

"Yeah."

"Then there ain't no laws around. Shit, fellers, we got this damned town to ourselfs."

Whispering, the bartender said to Levi, "Somebody ought to warn the bank. These yahoos look like robbers to me."

Levi only grunted. He knew these men. Knew about them. Had known too damned many of them. They were dangerous, no doubt about that. But he wanted no trouble. The bank could take care of itself. The whole damned sodbuster town could take care of itself. He had other things to worry about.

Draining his beer mug, he left, went to the stage and freight yards where his horse was kept, saddled up, and started out of town.

The stage and freight yards were on the west side. He rode east, down First Street. He saw the four gunsels come out of the saloon, staggering drunk, talking loud. Saw the young woman try to get around them on the street. Saw one of the toughs grab her by the arm.

Levi dismounted, dropped the reins, shifted his gun belt, and walked toward them. While he walked he wished he'd checked the loads on the Army Colt. But maybe he wouldn't need it. Hoped not.

"Please, sir, you're hurting my arm."

"Haw-haw, you're the only female I seen in this town that's worth lookin' twice at. Hows about a little feel?"

The young woman tried to pull free, but was no match for the tough. Where, Levi wondered, were the other men of Rockledge? Were they scared? Surely, they wouldn't just stand by and watch a woman get manhandled on the street.

"Please sir. Please let me go."

"Inna minute. Soon's I grab a feel."

Levi stepped between them, put his left hand in the middle of the tough's chest and shoved. Shoved hard. His jaws were clamped tight and his eyes were slits.

The gunsel staggered back four steps and stopped, standing spraddle-legged, his right hand near his gun butt. He hissed like a snake, "Why you skinny old pile of shit. Nobody pushes—"

He didn't get to finish what he'd started to say. Levi's experience told him that talking was useless. There was nothing to say anyway. He'd be a damned fool if he let this yahoo make the next move.

The Army Colt suddenly appeared in the old man's hand. Smoke and fire belched out of the bore at the same instant the gun barked. A .44 caliber lead ball smashed into the middle of the gunsel's chest. He fell back onto the seat of his pants, then flopped over on his side and lay still.

Three other hands grabbed for six-guns, but stopped suddenly when a shotgun boomed. Another gun popped halfway down the block. And from still another direction a man yelled, "Hold it right there."

The three gun hands froze. Three toughs looked around, looked at the bartender holding a double-barreled sixteen gauge, at the bank clerk down the strcct, pointing a long-barreled six-shooter at them, at Tudor Howell who'd come out of his store wearing an apron and carrying a repeating rifle.

They looked, shuffled their feet, and made certain their hands were well away from their guns. One of them stammered, "We—we didn't do nothin'. He did. I tried to talk 'im out of it, but he didn't listen."

"You was all together," the bartender said. His finger was on the second trigger of the shotgun, his thumb was on the second hammer.

"We was jist . . . I apologize, ma'am. We wasn't gonna let 'im hurt you."

Rubbing her arm, the young woman said nothing. Levi holstered the Army Colt. Howell said, "You men, whoever you are, get your horses, wherever they are, and get out of this town."

"Yeah, yessir. Our hosses're over at the freight pens. Yessir, we're goin' right now." The three walked down the middle of the street, leaving their partner lying in the street with a spot of blood in the center of his chest.

"Mister," Howell said, coming closer, "your name is Levi, isn't it?"

Levi's Adam's apple bobbed. "Yup."

"Well, Levi, I saw what happened. We all did. I'd have come sooner but I had to go get a gun. Anyway, we'll tell the sheriff all about it when he gets back, and you're in no trouble with the law."

"That's right," the bank clerk said. "There won't be no trouble over this."

The woman stepped in front of Levi. "I can't thank you enough, sir. I'm very grateful."

For the moment, the dead man was forgotten.

"Naw, you don't owe me, miss." He recognized her now. Though she wore a scarf over her blond hair, he recognized her as the pretty young woman who'd stood on the stage at the medicine show.

"But I do. If there is any way I can return the favor, just say so."

"Naw. These men wasn't gonna let 'im hurt you. I just happened to get here first, and I had a gun."

She held out her hand to shake, man-fashion. "My name is Ruth Ann Abraham, Mr. Levi. I'm an assistant to Dr. Woodrow. If you ever need anything, I'll be more than happy to oblige."

Taking only her fingertips in his calloused leathery hand, he shook once and let her hand drop. "Shore, miss. I'm acquainted with the doctor. Give 'im my regards."

"We'll take care of this carcass, Levi."

Riding down the wagon road, Levi had a feeling the town hadn't heard the last of the three gunslicks. They weren't bank robbers, but they were outlaws. If they'd come to rob the bank they'd gone about it all wrong. Levi knew how it should be done. Stay out of town.

Don't be seen. Rob the bank fast and quietly and get gone. Let them try to guess who did it.

No, they weren't bank robbers. They were cowboys gone bad. Cattle thieves. And with the boss of the C Bar hiding from the law and the hired hands leaving, C Bar cattle would be easy pickings.

Chapter Ten

Sleep was almost impossible in the cold night air. All Casey had to be thankful for was the dry weather. If he'd been wet he would have been even more miserable. He'd spent most of the night pacing, swinging his arms to keep the blood circulating. But now that the sun was up, he could sit down and rest.

Boy, he'd never again complain about hot weather. Nothing could feel better than that warm sun on his face. Nothing except some flapjacks and bacon or, hell, even cornmeal mush. Forget that, he told himself. Looking up at the granite walls on three sides of him, he saw two ravens flap overhead, and envied them. Must be great to fly like that. Ravens could eat almost anything. They stayed well fed the year around. Don't think about it. Soon he lay on his back in the tall grass and dozed.

Mounted on a fresh horse, Levi rode west into the foothills where he picked up a trail that joined the Glacier Trail into the high country. He was well fed. Mrs. Carter was still at the ranch and had fed him coffee, cured ham, toast, and plum preserves. They'd had a long talk.

"I'll stay as long as the groceries hold out," Mrs. Carter had said, settling her overweight body into a chair across the table. "Mrs. Casey hired me when I had nowhere else to turn, after my husband died in a snowslide up in the tall timbers. They treated me fine, and made sure I had ever'thing I need to do my work." She put her elbows on the table and her chin in her hands. "Mrs. Casey knew what hard work is. She told me about how her and Mr. Casey drove a hundred and fifty cows to this country from New Mexico Territory where she was raised. They homesteaded a hundred and sixty acres and built a one-room shack that they lived in for a long, long time. She told me how they sold calves and used the money to buy more cows, and how they spent their profits on cows and land instead of on lumber to build a house."

Levi had sipped his coffee and listened. Then he said, "Jim didn't talk much about how him and Mrs. Casey built this outfit, but I could guess. He worked just as hard as any hired man. Fact is, he worked harder. He wouldn't ask a hired man to work as hard as he did. And Mrs. Casey could fork a horse like a man and work like a man. She was somethin', wasn't she?"

"Yes, she was. Worked like a man but still ever' inch a lady. She could be elegant when she wanted to. I'm just thankful that she got to go up to Denver and stay in a fine hotel and eat in a fine restaurant and see some of those stage shows and do things like that before she was killed."

Thinking of her employer's death brought tears to Mrs. Carter's eyes. She stood and turned her back to Levi, trying to hide her tears.

Levi would never forget it. He'd heard about how Mrs. Casey had fed a small bunch of Indians who'd stopped at the ranch with their hands out. So when he

73

saw the five bucks riding west toward the mountains, about eight miles south of the ranch house, he'd thought nothing of it. He was alone, but they didn't bother him. Figuring they were going up to the high country to hunt, he went on about his work, using a team of harness horses and a fresno to dredge a dirt tank where water gathered in the wet seasons.

Not until his job was done and he was riding one harness horse and leading the other did he suspect that anything was wrong. When he'd ridden within sight of the ranch house he saw Mrs. Carter bending over something on the ground, waving her arms at him and screaming and crying. He booted the horse into a trot, slid off, and raised Mrs. Casey's head. Her eyes were open, and she was groaning. Then he saw the arrow buried deep in her left side.

Mrs. Carter was crying, "I tried to carry her in the house. I couldn't carry her. Take her in the house, Levi, and go fetch the doctor."

Levi had picked her up and placed her gently on a bed in the big bedroom. Mrs. Carter stopped crying long enough to fetch some scissors and cut her shirt away from the arrow. Mrs. Casey spoke in a pain-filled voice, "Where's Jim?"

"He rode north, Mrs. Casey. He oughtta be back purty soon. I'll go get that doctor in town. Uh, Mrs. Casey, think we oughtta try to pull that arrow out?"

Through clenched teeth, she said, "It has to come out."

"I'll try, ma'am." He knew only one way to do it. And he knew it would hurt like hell. When he took hold of the feathered shaft, he tried to talk to her, tried to get her mind off what he was doing. It didn't work. "I've seen arrows in men, Mrs. Casey, and I know they have to be pulled out right fast. You see, the Injuns tie them blades on with animal guts, and body heat loosens the bindin's, and if we don't pull 'er out now the shaft'll come off, and . . ."

Mrs. Carter was talking, "I seen 'em. I looked out of the kitchen window, and seen 'em ride up. Mrs. Casey was outside, and she talked to 'em a minute and she started to walk to the house. One of them savages put an arrow in his bow and shot her. They run off."

He couldn't do it. She didn't scream like most men would have, but she couldn't hold back the painful grunts. It was her face that stopped him—teeth grinding, features twisted, eyes squeezed shut.

"I'll fetch the doctor, ma'am. Maybe he's got something that'll keep it from hurtin' so much."

Within minutes he had a horse saddled and was riding as fast as the horse could run to Rockledge. At the same time he was pleading under his breath, Be there, doctor, be there. For God's sake be there.

That was three years ago this fall. Now, as he rode west, his horse climbing a steep trail that led to the Hatchet Lake Cow Camp, he remembered every second of it. She was the bravest woman he'd ever known, but it didn't save her life. Well, he couldn't do anything for her now. He tried to force it out of his mind and figure out what to do for her husband.

He knew when he saw the two cowboys in the yard in front of the one-room cabin that they'd heard. Otherwise, they'd be horseback somewhere, doing their work. The cabin and corral sat near a small glacier lake shaped like a hatchet blade, with a creek pouring out of it shaped like a hatchet handle. He could look back and see where the melting glacier had slid downhill a million years ago and plowed out a wide valley.

"Howdy, Buzz, Arnold," he said as he swung down.

"Howdy, Levi."

"I can tell by the look on your pans the sheriff was here."

"Yeah, him and a bunch of them town jaspers."

"Did he give you any trouble?"

"Oh," the lanky Buzz spoke with a drawl, "he tried to tell us what we know and what we don't know. We told him that what we know is nothin'."

"We didn't have to lie," the husky bowlegged Arnold said, pushing back a ragged black hat. "We didn't know nothin'."

"I reckon he told you all about everything."

"Yeah. Too bad. I always figgered the boss'd fight like a wildcat if he had to, but I can't see 'im just walkin' up to a man and shootin' 'im."

"He didn't. I was with 'im when that blabbermouth was shot."

"I never believed he did."

"You know," Levi said, "he's on the run now, and nobody else can sign your paychecks."

"We've been talkin' about that. We're about out of chuck here, and if we don't get some in a few days we'll have to ride out, quit the country."

Arnold said, "I'd buy some with my own money, but I only got a few bucks. Would you blame us, Levi, if we quit?"

"No. A man can't work without feedin' his face."

A man can't live without eating. How long does it take to starve? Casey recalled someone telling him once that the first few days were the worst. After that a man

76

didn't feel hunger. But after that a man got weaker fast. He'd have to do something soon.

Sneaking back to town and trying to steal something might work. If he prowled in the dark long enough he might find a house where nobody was at home, go in and help himself. Dangerous, but better than starving.

But, lord, it would be embarrassing if he was caught.

No, best thing to do was walk to the Hatchet Lake Cow Camp. The sheriff had been there and gone by now. The two cowboys, Buzz and Arnold, would share what chuck they had. If they were still there. Come to think of it, they were about out of groceries, too. He was planning to send Levi up there with a pack horse load. Should have done that. Would have if he hadn't been convicted and locked up.

Well, surely there was something to eat up there. If Buzz and Arnold had pulled out, they'd surely left something. Stale biscuits. Moldy bacon. Something. He'd give it another day, then he'd have to move. He'd have to walk on the Glacier Trail or take a different route and climb hand over hand in places. There was buck brush on the lower end of the trail and willow bushes on the high end to hide behind if he saw anybody coming. Another cold night, then move.

Levi had been riding since sunup. He'd skirted the town to get into the foothills, but by midafternoon he'd found no sign of Jim Casey. That was good news as well as bad. If he couldn't cut Jim's sign the sheriff couldn't either. He had two blankets and a seven-foot length of canvas rolled up behind his cantle, and he had two saddlebags filled with groceries.

He didn't bring an extra horse because if he was seen leading a saddled horse any lame brain could figure out what he was up to. When he found Jim he'd bring him a horse at night.

Riding in and out of the arroyos, up and down, he studied the ground, the high hills, the lower hills. The sheriff and his bunch had been to both cow camps, and the sheriff would probably go back. He might guess that Jim had stayed out of sight of the camps for a few days, but was forced by hunger and cold to get inside one of them. The Hatchet Lake camp was the closer. The sheriff could ride up there for a surprise visit, hoping to catch Jim unawares.

Be patient, Jim, he said under his breath. Stay put. I'll find you.

Suddenly, he reined up, sat his saddle, and scratched his wrinkled, leathery jaw. He said aloud, "Well now, why in hell didn't I think of that before."

All right, Jim Casey said to himself, one more day. I'm still strong enough to walk uphill, and it wouldn't do to leave here too soon. One more night won't kill me. He'd walked enough to test his legs, but no more than that. Save your strength, he'd said. Now he was sitting on the ground, staring at the sky. High thin clouds were moving overhead, but they didn't look much like rain clouds. Though it was midafternoon, the sun had gone behind the canyon wall on the west. Trouble with a damned canyon, he thought, is the sun doesn't shine more than a few hours a day. He lay back and started to doze.

Then he sat up, wide awake, listening. Somebody or something was coming. It was close to the ground, moving slowly, carefully in the brush.

Another trouble with a canyon: no place to run.

Eyes and ears straining, feeling like a trapped animal, Casey watched.

Whatever was coming was coming right up the middle of the scrubs. Casey walked quietly to the south edge and squatted against a granite cliff where he could duck into the brush if need be. He watched. He waited.

Chapter Eleven

A face appeared in the scrub oaks. A lean, wrinkled face under a brown hat. It looked. It said, "Jim? Are you here, Jim?"

Casey stood. "I'm over here."

Levi crawled on his hands and knees out of the brush, sat on his haunches and grinned. "Well, don't this beat all? You go pokin' around and you run into the dangdest people."

Grinning, too, Casey said, "You're not the most handsome animal I ever saw, but if you brought some chuck I'll put up with you."

"I got two saddle pockets stuffed full and some blankets and a skillet and a little coffeepot. I didn't bring a horse 'cause I didn't wanta be seen leadin' a horse. And oh yeah, I brought you a gun. I asked Mrs. Carter to look in your bedroom for a gun and she found one that looks exactly like the one you been packin'. And a hat. I seen your hat hangin' in the sheriff's office."

"I've got a pair of those guns. Bought them in Denver. Navy Colts fixed to fire metal cartridges."

"This'n looks like it's never been used. The holster looks new, too."

"I've never carried more than one at a time."

"Well," Levi tried to joke, "I'll run to the market across the street and fetch you somethin' to eat. I'll bring a horse later, in the dark."

"Look out for the street cars."

"I'll be right back." Grinning again, Levi said, "Don't run off nowheres." He backed into the brush and disappeared.

Levi left his horse tied to an oak branch and crawled back to Jim, carrying his saddlebags. Sitting cross-legged on the ground, Jim ate dried beef and tomatoes from two tin cans. Immediately, he felt stronger. "Wouldn't do to build a fire in the daylight," he said. "You could see the smoke for a good many miles. But right after dark I'm gonna make some coffee and fry some bacon and eat like a man is supposed to eat. Anything new, Levi?"

The old man told him about the shooting on First Street and explained that at least three witnesses told Sheriff Waltham Jackson what had happened. "The sheriff ain't gonna make no fuss over it." Then he took Amos P. Sharp's check out of a shirt pocket and explained that.

"I'll sign it. He thinks I'll get a new trial, huh?"

"That's what he says. But he said it'll take time and money."

"Yeah. Time. I like to see the country civilized and a good legal system and all, but the legal way takes too damn much time. And it costs too damn much money."

"Whatta you figger on doin', Jim?"

"I've been thinking and thinking, and I don't know. That woman, that Agnes Mooreman, lied in court. She knows she lied. I wonder what else she knows."

"Might stick a gun barrel up her nose and ask 'er."

"No. I don't want you to do anything. Just keep your ears open. Besides, you wouldn't threaten a woman."

"Never have. But if it came down to you or her, I'd made her dirty them holy-roller drawers of hers."

"Don't touch her, Levi." Casey was silent a moment, thinking. "I've got another problem. In fact, I'm breaking out with problems. You say everybody has quit? There's nobody at the cow camps or at the ranch?"

"Just me and Mrs. Carter. When the word gets out, and it will, the cow thieves'll help theirselfs."

"That's for sure. And I've got a bank note coming due. Somehow, I've got to round up about three hundred head and get them to market to pay off the bank."

"You and me can handle that many cattle down on the prairie, but you ain't got that many down there. You tell me what to do and I'll do 'er."

"Got any ideas yourself?"

"Buzz and Arnold left about twenty horses up at Hatchet Lake. I can unroll my bed up there and start pushin' cattle down. It'll take some time and hard ridin', but with that many horses I can do 'er."

"I've got 'till October. With the two of us riding, we can gather a lot of cattle by then."

"But you gotta stay outta sight. That sheriff's a tricky sumbuck. He'll ride up to the cow camps and to the rancho at times when he thinks nobody is expectin' 'im."

"Yeah, he will. And at the same time I've got to try to find out who killed Reverend Weems."

Shaking his head, Levi said, "What we need, Jim, is a friend in town. Somebody with big ears."

"Add to that a big curiosity."

Mrs. Agnes Mooreman was embarrassed. Only one person since her husband's death had seen her naked.

Here she was lying on the doctor's examination table with her dress up around her breasts and her bloomers down around her knees. Could the doctor tell? Did it show? She tried to cover her most private parts with her hands, but the doctor gently removed her hands and continued probing her stomach. He pushed on her with his fingertips and listened through a wooden device he called a stethoscope. He put the newfangled thing down and put his ear to her bare stomach. She tried to read the expression on his face, but his expression told her nothing. Well, at least she'd taken a bath the night before. Thank goodness for that. But how embarrassing.

Dr. Woodrow was thanking goodness, too. He was thankful that he'd hired Ruth Ann Abraham and had a healthy woman in the examination room. He'd always felt uncomfortable examining women. Somehow, having a woman assistant in the room made it easier. He straightened up, put the stethoscope on top of his instrument chest.

"Please get dressed now, Mrs. Mooreman."

Quickly, the patient slid off the table and pulled her bloomers up and her dress down. "What's wrong with me, Doctor? Did you find anything wrong?"

"Mrs. Mooreman." Dr. Woodrow wore a somber expression, looking directly at the patient's face. "You should by all means go to a hospital." He was tired of telling patients that, but it was his duty to give them the best advice. "You should go very soon."

A look of fear came over the woman's face. "Why? What's wrong? Tell me what's wrong with me."

"Mrs. Mooreman, you have a tumor in your stomach." He added quickly, "It can be removed by surgery."

"What . . . what if it's not removed?"

"It would be fatal."

"Oh . . . oh." Her knees buckled and she started to fall. Moving fast, Ruth Ann was behind her, helping the doctor to hold her up. When the patient was steady, Ruth Ann quickly brought a chair over for her to sit on. "Oh . . . I'm going to die."

"Not necessarily, Mrs. Mooreman," Dr. Woodrow said. "The tumor can be removed."

"But . . . but I've heard of people dying of tumors."

Silently, the doctor admitted to himself that most stomach tumors were fatal, but his duty now was to give the patient hope. "Many tumors have been removed successfully. You have to have faith, Mrs. Mooreman."

"But . . . a hospital. In Denver. I . . . I don't want to go to a hospital."

"Mrs. Mooreman, stomach surgery is a major operation. You need a general anesthetic. Hospitals have excellent equipment. There are some very good surgeons in Denver."

"How . . . how long do I have to live?"

"It's impossible to predict. You could live a year without surgery. But you will be uncomfortable."

"Can't you do it, Dr. Woodrow? I don't want to die in a hospital."

"Yes, but you will need care beyond surgery. A hospital has trained nurses."

Mrs. Mooreman summoned her courage, her strength, and stood. "I want you to do it. I have friends who will care for me. How soon can you do it?"

"Whenever you are ready. But again, I strongly recommend a hospital."

"No. I will prepare myself. I must go to church and pray. I must confess my sins. Then I will be ready."

Ruth Ann asked, "Your sins, Mrs. Mooreman?" Then

she wished she hadn't. Asking that question was unprofessional.

"Not in the eyes of God, but ... oh, how I miss the Reverend Weems." She drew herself up. "We still have a small church with an altar. Thank God for that."

Ruth Ann was curious, but she said no more. Not until after the patient had gone, did she mention it. "That woman is a sinner? That self-righteous, God-fearing woman?"

With a wry grin, the doctor said, "She and the Reverend Weems were very close, you know."

"You don't suppose ... ? She is fairly attractive, and the reverend was single. You don't suppose they could have ... ?"

The doctor shrugged. "Who knows. It's none of my concern. She did testify in the murder trial and her testimony was damaging to the defendant, Jim Casey."

A puzzle-frown brought a squint to Ruth Ann's eyes. "Curious, isn't it? I wonder if she lied."

"I have no way of knowing. But ..." Dr. Woodrow studied the floor a moment, rubbing the back of his neck. "I wanted to say something more when I testified, but I didn't get a chance. Hmm. It's probably not important, but the prosecutor did seem to think it was important that I tell about the gunpowder burns on the body."

"What was it you wanted to say? You know by now that I have a wicked curiosity about everything and everybody."

"Well, the shirt the reverend was wearing had caught fire. It definitely had burned for a second or two around the bullet hole."

"Hmm." The puzzle-frown deepened. "I wonder if

that means anything? Did you mention this to the sheriff?"

"No. I know nothing about firearms. Perhaps I should
have mentioned it to the sheriff."

"Curious, isn't it?"

Chapter Twelve

They didn't bring their horses through the scrub brush, knowing big animals would leave a trail that could be seen by anyone riding past. They didn't need to bring them into the granite pocket anyway. When Levi came back, leading a saddled horse and a pack horse, Jim Casey was ready to ride.

A quarter moon put out enough light that they could easily find their way up the glacier trail. They'd been up that trail, along Glacier Creek, so many times they could have found their way in total darkness. About halfway up, they passed a half-dozen dark shapes, moving shapes, and Levi commented:

"There's some we won't have to push down."

"I wish they'd come down farther south. We can't gather a herd of cattle anywhere near town."

"Well, maybe their tracks will cover ours."

"There's that." They rode silently, then Casey asked, "How come you didn't put my saddle on this horse, Levi?"

"That harness maker was one of the bunch that come out to the rancho with the sheriff, and he recognized your saddle. I figgered if the sheriff goes back and sees your outfit gone he'll get suspicious."

"Good thinking."

They found the Hatchet Lake camp deserted. Levi struck a match and lit a coal oil lamp. Together, they unloaded the pack horse and carried groceries and Levi's bedroll into the cabin. "At least Buzz and Arnold left the place fairly clean," Casey allowed. Looking around, he said, "Boy, they were plumb out of chuck. Can't say I blame them for quitting."

"There's two bunks here, Jim. You might as well spend the rest of the night in here."

"I've been thinking about that. If the sheriff comes along and sees two beds in use, he'll know I'm somewhere near. And if I sleep out in the timber, he might find my bed out there, too.

"He will if he does enough ridin' and lookin', but I'm bettin' he won't look no further than this shack."

"That's what I was thinking. My chances are better if I sleep out in the sticks."

Levi unsaddled the horses and fed them some of what little hay was left. While he did that, Casey mixed some pancake batter and fried bacon. They ate well, then Casey carried his bed into the pine forest that bordered the lake on two sides. He guessed he'd get an hour and a half of sleep before daylight.

Hoofbeats awakened him. Sitting up in his blankets, he saw Levi running in the horses left behind by the two hired cowboys. Levi brought the horses in on the run, knowing that was the easiest way to handle horses that knew where they were supposed to go. If he'd let them walk they would have wandered. Inside the pole corral near the cabin, the horses snorted and blew dust and pollen from their nostrils.

"They're all here," Levi said after he'd shut the corral gate. "Twenty of 'em. That ought to keep us horseback."

"I see Buzz and Arnold left the shoeing tools and shoes. Looks like they took no more than what belonged to them."

"They're honest," Levi said.

"Wish I could have paid them and kept them."

Hastily, they ate more flapjacks and bacon, guzzled some coffee, then saddled two fresh horses and rode south. They left the corral gate open so the horses could graze in a twenty-five-acre horse pasture. The pasture fence, built four years earlier by Casey and three hired hands, was part crossbuck poles, part plain wire, part stacked tree trunks, and part lake front.

It was close to noon before they saw any sign of cattle. Casey was getting worried. Had the cattle drifted that far from Hatchet Lake? Two buck deer and three does bounded like rubber balls across a small grassy park ahead of them. Both men noted the two-day-old cattle sign and saw that the grass in the park had been grazed on, but there were no cattle.

"See horse tracks, Levi?"

"Yeah. I wonder. Buzz and Arnold have been gone for four days now."

"What does this tell you?"

"It tells me, Jim, that somebody else is gatherin' C Bar stock."

"I figure three or four riders. What do you think?"

"I think there's three. And I'll bet I've met those gents before."

"Those hardcases in Rockledge?"

"Them. There was four and now there's three."

"There are cows and some of this year's calf crop, and some yearlings, too. About twenty-five head."

"Yup. Can't of gone too far yet."

"Bet they're going over the divide with 'em. They can find a market over there."

"They got word that nobody is ridin' this country. It's all over the county now that your hired help quit and you're runnin' from the law."

"They didn't waste any time."

Levi shifted in his saddle, pushed his hat back, and scratched his nearly bald head. "Well, with three men drivin' twenty-five cattle through these timbers and over these rocks, they ain't goin' any further'n they have to, and they ain't watchin' their back trail."

"No. As far as they know there's not a man within twenty miles." Casey drew the Navy Colt and checked the cylinder. "Whatta you say, Levi, let's catch up with them and burn their asses a little."

"I checked the loads on my cannon soon's I got outta bed this mornin'. We're gonna have to lope to catch 'em before dark."

Touching spurs to his horse, Casey said, "Let's lope."

A tonsillectomy was routine in a hospital. In a doctor's examination room it was not so routine. The main problem was keeping the patient unconscious without overdosing him. Chloroform could be dangerous. Too little and the patient would wake up screaming. Too much and the patient could stop breathing. Dr. Woodrow used an inhaler, a cylinder with a tube for each nostril. He dropped the chloroform into a cotton wad inside the cylinder a drop at a time, carefully. He watched with satisfaction as the boy's eyelids slowly closed.

The boy's mother was at the head of the table, talking, "You've been whinin' for weeks about a sore throat and now we're gonna do somethin' about it so quit your whinin'. Be quiet, Horace."

Ruth Ann was holding the boy's wrist, checking the pulse. "Still steady," she reported. Certain now that the boy was unconscious, Dr. Woodrow pried the mouth wide open and used a metal speculum to hold it open. He took a short-handled scalpel from a pot of boiling water, then looked at Ruth Ann. "Steady," she said.

"Mrs. Doty," Dr. Woodrow said, "will you please step back now. This will only take a minute."

A minute was all it took. The doctor removed the tissue, dropped it into a bucket, and immediately covered the bucket. He swabbed the throat with carbolic and water, then removed the tubes from the boy's nostrils.

"He's going to have a sore throat for a few days, Mrs. Doty. He won't be able to eat anything. Give him all the milk he can drink, and you might mix some bread with the milk. I'll give you some bromide to help him sleep and some laudanum. Give him the laudanum only if the pain is severe."

After instructing the mother on how to mix the bromide and laudanum, the doctor took off his white coat and washed his hands thoroughly in warm water. By then the boy was regaining consciousness. "His pulse is strong," Ruth Ann said. "He's a strong boy."

"I think he'll be fine, Mrs. Doty. Do you have a buggy?"

"No, but my husband'll be here purty soon and he'll carry 'im home. I cain't carry 'im. Lord knows I've got enough to do, what with three more young'uns and a husband to feed, but with the Lord's help I'll bear it."

"Fine. If you need me don't hesitate to send for me. Miss Abraham will call on you every day for a while to see how he is doing."

The boy was crying quietly now. The mother scolded him, "Quit yer cryin', Horace. Yer poppa'll be here purty soon and he don't like to hear you cry." Ruth Ann touched his cheek with her fingertips. "For a six-year-old you're a brave boy, Horace. It will hurt for a while, but it will get well, and you'll get well, and you'll feel better than you've felt in a long time. Won't that be grand?"

Walking to Mrs. Spencer's boarding house, Ruth Ann carried two gunny sacks, each a quarter full of potatoes and turnips. With a sack in each hand she had to stop and rest twice during the three-block walk. Mrs. Spencer was happy to get the produce, and was even happier when Ruth Ann said she had to return to the doctor's house to fetch a quarter of beef that a patient had given him.

At supper, the six boarders dined on baked beef ribs and potatoes and gravy. Two of the boarders were women—Ruth Ann and a middle-aged woman who taught grades one through six in the one-room school. Unlike cowboys who ate silently, the boarders talked. And talked.

"Is it true, Ruth Ann, that Mrs. Mooreman has a tumor in her stomach?"

"Why, uh, you know it would be unprofessional of me to talk about one of our patients. Her condition is confidential, you know." Silently, she wondered how the word got out. "Why do you ask?"

"She told somebody that told somebody else that told me."

"Well, I just can't comment."

"She's spent a lot of time in church lately," the schoolteacher said. "She wants to be sure she's right with the Lord."

"She's always spent a lot of time at church," Mrs. Spencer said. "And in Reverend Weems's house."

"And Reverend Weems spent a lot of time in her house."

Ruth Ann listened, but said nothing.

They were gaining fast. The tracks and droppings told them that. "Ain't easy to drive a bunch of cattle through the timber and willers," Levi allowed. They broke out of a pine forest and looked across a wide vega where granite boulders stuck up out of the earth in places but where no trees grew. "They spent the night here," Casey allowed. "Took them a while to get the cattle gathered and moving again this morning."

Levi got down and adjusted his saddle. "Damn rimfire riggins're good for goin' downhill, but not so good for goin' uphill."

"They're making breast collars now for rimfire riggings that crawl back on a horse."

Squinting at the western horizon, Levi said, "Know what I'm thinkin', Jim?"

"I'm thinking the same thing."

"Yup. Best place to get over the divide is four or five mile south of here. Bad place to drive a bunch of cattle, and they'll have to go around, but we can do some climbin' and maybe get there ahead of 'em."

"Do you remember a game trail that goes up there?" Casey pointed to a rocky ridge. "If my memory serves me right, it goes south from the top."

"I re'clect it. Ain't too bad a trail."

"Let's get up there."

It took an hour and a half to ride to the top of the ridge. At places, the game trail petered out, and they had to traverse the hill, almost doubling back on themselves. They rode through tall spruce and pine and around granite boulders as big as castles. About every ten minutes they had to stop and let their horses blow. At the top, finally, they picked up the trail made by deer and elk, and followed it along the top until it went down the other side of the ridge.

"Guess my memory isn't so good," Casey said. "I thought the trail went on south."

"We can make it. We ain't far from where them thieves have to start climbin'."

"Do I hear cattle bawling?"

Levi listened. "Shore 'nuff. Mother cows that lost track of their calves."

"We'll get there ahead of them, all right."

"And that," Levi said, "is where the shootin' starts."

"Are you ready to risk your life, Levi, for somebody else's cattle?"

"Jim." The older man fixed his squinty eyes on his employer. "I always figgered you was one of the smartest fellers I ever knew, but that was a dumb question."

Grinning, Casey said, "You're right. After all that's happened since I hired you . . . that question was downright stupid."

Chapter Thirteen

Traveling wasn't easy on top of the ridge. The country dropped sharply. Huge boulders sat in jumbled piles and hung over the top, looking like a hard push would send them crashing to the bottom.

"Ever figger out, Jim, how them big rocks got like that? Looks like The Creator or somethin' just piled 'em there."

"I read someplace that they were once one big rock, bigger than three or four barns, and the weather split them open. You know, freezing and thawing. Given enough time—and they had probably a million years—that could cause them to break up in smaller pieces. Then the wind and rain rounded off the edges. Can you believe that?"

"Yup. Ever'thing's bound to change in a million years."

"If my memory isn't playing tricks on me again, we're getting close to where they're going to have to turn the cattle uphill."

"Yup." Levi tried to joke, tried to get his mind off the gun battle that was ahead. "For a second there I thought you was gonna try to remember back a million years."

"Don't think I can reach back that far." Casey was feeling a little nervous, too, but refused to show it.

"Me neither. I was purty young then."

They could see the cattle now. They'd guessed right. About twenty-five head. A mixed herd. Cows, calves, yearlings, and two bulls. All but one of the cattle were longhorns with a mixture of colors. One of the bulls was a nearly white shorthorn. Not only did it have shorter horns, it also had shorter legs. But the legs carried almost twice as much beef as did the legs on the longhorns. He was one of a half-dozen shorthorn bulls Jim had bought a year earlier to see what kind of calves they would get. And to see if they could survive outside a farm feedlot.

"What I'd like to do," Jim said, "is catch them before they get very far up this way. Gunfire will stampede the cattle, and if they run downhill they'll be going where we want them to go."

"Yeah. If we can do that, them gunsels will've done some of our work for us."

They went on, then: "See that pile of boulders, Levi? I think we can get behind it without them seeing us."

"Good spot, all right. They havta come right by there. What'll we do, Jim, kill them three?"

"I'd rather not kill anybody today. If we do we'll have to bury the bodies, and we haven't got a shovel. Besides, we'd have to report it to the sheriff, and I don't want anything to do with the sheriff right now."

"Throw enough lead their way and maybe they'll run."

"That's what I'm hoping. I don't think they'll make much of a fight of it."

They worked their way down to the boulders, hobbled their horses out of sight. Casey picked a spot at one end of the pile of boulders and Levi hunkered down at the other end. Six-guns in hand, they waited.

The herd was coming. Three riders yelled, whistled,

and cursed, driving twenty-five cattle uphill, through a scattering of pines. They're working hard for free money, Casey thought. Levi was thinking the same thing. Better than working for wages, though. He knew all about it. A man could work all his life for twenty-five a month and chuck and die of old age without a dime in his pockets.

Levi had been up the trail from South Texas to Wichita, knew what a long, hard, dangerous job it was, knew what it was like to leave Wichita with nothing to show for it except maybe a new pair of britches. Knew how a man could get to thinking of easier ways to get money.

Everybody hated a thief, but if a man wanted to steal somebody else's cattle or rob a bank he could find an excuse. A man could think of an excuse for almost anything if he wanted to.

They were coming. He was glad the boss didn't want to kill them. He'd been one of them.

Now he could see their faces. Yep, it was them three. They should have got some help and rounded up a bigger bunch of cattle. Levi hunkered down closer to the ground and waited for the boss to fire the first shot.

From where he was Casey could see Levi and knew he was waiting for him to shoot first. Now was the time. He cocked the hammer back on the .36 caliber Colt, pointed it at the sky, and squeezed the trigger.

The loud POP of the exploding cartridge bounced off the ridge and rolled across the narrow valley below. Casey fired another shot. Then Levi fired, his heavier caliber Colt booming like a cannon.

The three riders stopped. They looked uphill at where the shots had come from. Levi fired again, sending a lead ball close enough to one of the riders that he could hear it go past. Cattle turned in their tracks and scattered, running downhill. Casey expected the three men to turn tail themselves and ride for safety.

But they didn't run.

One of them cursed, dropped off his horse, and snapped a shot at Casey's head. It was close, screaming off a boulder. The man cocked his gun and was ready to fire again. Levi sent a lead ball his way, missing the man but hitting the ground near his feet.

Now the other two were on the ground and firing, firing as fast as they could cock their pistols, aim and squeeze the triggers. Lead was spanging off the boulders and whining off into space.

Goddam, Levi said under his breath, this tryin' to scare 'em off ain't workin'.

Why in hell don't they just run for it? Casey asked himself. Do they think they can outshoot us, kill us, then go on with their plan?

The three had found cover now. One behind a tree and the other two behind boulders.

Five guns were firing, sounding like one continuous ear-punishing roar. Casey's Colt clicked on empty. Hastily, he took six cartridges from his shell belt, punched out the empties, and reloaded. Two shots came close enough to shatter granite two feet from his face. Glancing at Levi, he saw the old man pouring black powder from a powder horn into the cylinder of his big pistol, and knew it would take him longer to reload.

One of the men down there also saw Levi reloading and believed he had a chance to get close enough to the old man to kill him. Bending low he ran toward Levi. Casey got him in his gunsights, squeezed off a shot.

The man spun half-around, dropped his gun, and grabbed his right side.

Shoot to scare, hell, Casey thought. This is getting downright serious. He fired at the gunsel behind a tree, saw chips fly off the tree a few inches above the man's head. At the same time another bullet spanged off a boulder near Casey's right shoulder.

Now Levi was firing again, his old black powder pistol booming. The injured man was leaving, holding his right side with one hand and trying to get on a gun-shy horse with the other. One of his partners ran over to hold the horse for him. Then the man behind the tree ran for his horse.

While Levi conserved his shots, Casey kept it up, burning the air around them, knowing he could reload if he needed to.

The three were horseback now, riding at a gallop back the way they'd come. Casey left his cover and stood in the open, watching them. He saw with satisfaction that the cattle had scattered. It would take three men too long to gather them again. They wouldn't try.

The fight was over.

"Levi. Are you hurt?"

"Naw." The old man stood. "For a minute there I thought we was gonna have to fight for our lives."

"They didn't give up as easy as I thought they would. Where do you think they'll go?"

"Not to Rockledge. Prob'ly to Jack's Corners where the railroad is." Levi walked up to Casey, pushed open the cylinder of his Army Colt, and reached for the powder horn hanging from his belt. "They'll tank up on old Jack's whiskey, and figger out what kind of theivin' to try next."

"The one I shot, how did he look to you?"

"Hard to tell. Took a ball in the side, but he was ridin'. Might die and might not."

"Well, at least we won't have to bury him or report anything to the law."

Looking at the sky and the rocky ridge to the west,

Levi allowed, "Be dark in a couple hours. Them three was plannin' to get over the divide before dark."

"They seemed to think they had all the time in the world. Probably thought there wasn't a man left on the C Bar."

"That's what they figgered on."

"We're closer to the Indian Creek camp now. Whatta you say, let's spend the night there instead of going back to Hatchet Lake."

"It's gonna be dark before we get to either one of 'em. We can catch some fresh horses at Indian Creek in the mornin' and round up them cattle and get 'em started driftin' down."

"Yeah. That's twenty-five head. All we need is another two hundred and seventy-five."

They went to their horses, removed the soft horsehair hobbles, and mounted. "Whatta think we can do, Jim, after we get that many cattle together? Drive 'em to Jack's Corners and load 'em on rail cars?"

"If I'm lucky, I can find a buyer in Denver who'll take them from there. Bring his own crew."

"Will you get as much for 'em thataway?"

"No. I could get more on delivery, but maybe I'll get enough to pay off the bank. That's my main worry now."

Riding downhill, the two got their horses into a trot, and at the bottom of the ridge turned south to the C Bar's Indian Creek Cow Camp. The sun went behind the ridge, and its light reflected off thin clouds, creating bright streaks of red and blue. The colors changed slowly until the sun put out no more light. Then it was dark.

Riding side by side in the dark, staying on a cattle trail that paralleled Indian Creek, both men were deep in thought, thinking about how difficult it would be for two men to gather three hundred cattle in the high country and drive them down onto the prairie. Finally, Levi spoke:

"Know somethin', Jim? I've worked for other fellers all my life—well, most of my life—and I've heard hired hands bellyache about low wages and half-broke horses and beans for ever' meal, but somehow we never gave much thought to the bosses' troubles. We knew we'd get paid, but you bosses could get wiped out by a dry summer or a hard winter and get nothin'. You never know if you're gonna make a profit or go bust."

Jim chuckled in the dark. "That's business. But a cowman is the most optimistic breed in the world. A sodbuster has a couple of dry summers, and he loads his wagon, gathers his wife and kids, and moves on. A cowman is too damned stubborn. If we get wiped out we borrow from the bank, restock, and hope for better times."

"So you always have to worry about payin' off the bank."

"There's always that. We bought land with what we borrowed, and we figured that no matter what mother nature throws at us, we'll have our land."

"Uh-huh."

"But what we didn't figure on was taxes. Now that Colorado is a state, and the General Assembly has created Oak County, our taxes have doubled. We could be taxed to death." Casey talked matter-of-factly, without rancor. "The more government the more taxes."

"Uh-huh. That's somethin' us hired hands never had to worry about."

They rode silently until Levi said, "Camp's not far ahead. There's nobody there, but maybe they left some chuck."

"How many horses have we got at Indian Creek?"

"Eighteen. Good horses."

The Indian Creek cabin was only a big dark blob among a scattering of tall pines, and the two men worked by feel, unsaddling and hobbling their horses near the creek where the grass was good.

Rusty hinges creaked as they opened the cabin door. Neither man smoked, but they always carried wooden matches. Casey struck a match and let out a groan. The room had been ransacked. Flour and cornmeal had been spilled from cloth bags, and pots and pans had been thrown onto the floor. The two lamps in the cabin were smashed. Levi swore when he struck a match and saw the damage.

"They were here," Casey said, "and I'll be surprised if they left anything to eat."

Striking more matches, they prowled through the room, searching the wooden coffee crate nailed to a wall and used for a cupboard, searching the cabin for anything useful.

"I've been hungry before, Levi. Can you stand to miss a couple more meals?"

"Yup."

"I might as well sleep in here tonight. If the sheriff comes up this way he won't get here too early in the morning. Not unless he's camping somewhere around here."

"He ain't. I'd bet on it."

"What we'll have to do is, you go back to Hatchet Lake and fetch some groceries from there. While you're doing that I'll see how many cattle I can gather. The Indian Creek Trail comes out south of town, and that's as good a place as any to hold a herd."

"Yup. That's what I'll do."

But that's not the way it happened.

At daylight, while Casey scrounged through what little was left of the flour and baking soda, trying to find enough to mix some pancake batter, Levi saddled his horse and went out to wrangle in the remuda. When he came back without a herd of horses, Casey guessed what had happened.

"Gone, huh?"

"Stole. Ever' one of 'em."

Casey swore. He sat on a bunk and swore. Then he stood. "We'd better get back to Hatchet Lake before they steal everything there. And before we starve."

"Know what worries me most, Jim?"

"Yeah. I thought it was the three gunsels we drove off yesterday, but it wasn't. They had stolen cattle but no horses. Somebody else was here."

"Yup. There's more than one gang of thieves."

Chapter Fourteen

Ruth Ann tried to sound cheerful. "We're ready, Mrs. Mooreman. Are you ready?"

"Yes." The patient had shaved her pubis the night before as directed by the doctor, and now she lay on the examination table, covered with a clean white sheet. Dr. Woodrow's instruments were in a pot of boiling water. The doctor was in his kitchen, thoroughly washing his hands.

"It will be over soon, Mrs. Mooreman."

"I made my confessions to the Good Lord, and if I don't wake up, I'm ready to meet Him."

"Your confessions, Mrs. Mooreman?"

"Yes. I don't think what the reverend and I did was a sin, but I asked forgiveness anyway. We prayed together before and after, and it was beautiful, truly beautiful."

"Oh, I see." Then Ruth Ann's curiosity got the better of her. "Mrs. Mooreman, did you tell the truth in the murder trial?"

"I did not lie. What I said was the truth as best as I remember."

"Did Mr. Casey threaten the reverend?"

"He was very angry. He accused the reverend of lying. The Reverend Weems did not lie."

"But did he threaten the reverend?"

"Well, he might have. He was angry enough. I believe he did."

"But you're not sure?"

"I don't recall the exact words, but I do recall that he was angry, and he always carried a gun."

"But—" Ruth Ann didn't get to finish her question.

"All right," Dr. Woodrow said, "Ruth Ann put the inhaler in place, will you please. Mrs. Mooreman, you are going to take a nap. You will have pleasant dreams."

With the inhaler in place, tubes in the patient's nostrils, Ruth Ann began dropping liquid chloroform into the cotton inside the inhaler's cylinder. It took a few minutes, but fumes from the chloroform had the patient drowsy, and finally sound asleep.

"How's her pulse?"

Feeling for the jugular vein in the patient's throat, Ruth Ann said, "Strong."

Dr. Woodrow pulled the gauze mask up over his mouth and nose, pulled the sheet down, exposing the patient's nakedness, and took a razor-sharp surgical knife from the pot of boiling water.

While he worked, Ruth Ann continued feeding chloroform into the inhaler cylinder a slow drop at a time. When the doctor looked at her, she felt the pulse and answered, "It's slowed a little, but still good."

He worked silently, and his assistant didn't disturb him with questions or comments. Every ten seconds, she checked the pulse. Finally, Dr. Woodrow took the tumor out of the patient's stomach and dropped it into the bucket near his feet. Only then did he speak, voice partially muffled through the mask:

"It wasn't as big as I thought it was. I think I got all of it."

"Does it look like the kind that will spread?"

"Can't tell. Only time will tell. Got to sew her up now."

Not a man was in sight when Sheriff Waltham Jackson rode up to the C Bar headquarters. A few horses grazed nearby, but there were none in the corrals. He rode up to the house, noted that there were still clean curtains in the windows, and the porch had been swept recently.

"Hello, the house," he yelled. He yelled it twice before he saw a face peering from a window. Then the front door opened and Mrs. Carter stood in it.

"Mornin', Mizz Carter. Fine mornin', isn't it?"

The hired housekeeper and cook spoke warily, "Good mornin', sheriff. Are you lookin' for somebody again?"

"Yes, ma'am, I am. Mind if I get down?"

"You can get down and come in the house if you want to."

He tied his horse to a hitch rail near the front door and followed her into the kitchen. She put a coffeepot on the stove.

"You here alone, Mizz Carter?"

"Yes. The men done quit 'cause they couldn't get their pay. All but old Levi, and he went up to one of the cow camps. Don't know when he'll be back."

"Don't reckon you've seen anything of your boss?"

"I haven't seen him and I don't know where he is, and that's a fact."

"Hmm. Mind if I sit down? The coffee's perkin'."

"Sit. I'll pour you a cup. Ain't got no cream, now that old Levi ain't here to milk the jersey cow. He turned her out with her calf 'till he gets back."

"Are you plannin' to stay here, Mizz Carter?"

"Yes. As long as I can."

"Might be kinda dangerous for a woman alone. I think everybody in the county knows by now that the hired help has gone."

"I know how to shoot. My late husband showed me how and made me practice, rest his soul." She poured a cup of coffee and set it before him at the kitchen table.

"It's still dangerous, but it's your decision. Mind if I look around? After I drink this coffee, that is."

"Look around all you want to. Can't you do something to keep the stealers away? You're the sheriff, and all."

Sheriff Jackson took a sip of coffee and shook his head. "Wish I could, but I've got only one deputy and we can't stand guard out here all the time." He took another sip and used his fingers to wipe a drop of coffee off his upper lip. "As a matter of fact, Mizz Carter, I'd advise you to go to town. I'll help you catch some horses and hitch one to a buggy if you want."

"I'm not goin'."

On his way back to Rockledge, Sheriff Jackson wasn't happy with the way things had turned out. The C Bar would go to pieces now. The thieves would help themselves. What was one of the best and biggest cattle ranches in Colorado would be stripped clean by thieves, and what was left would be sold for back taxes. Or go to a bank somewhere. Most cattlemen were in hock up to their asses to the banks. Too bad about Jim Casey.

Sheriff Jackson, Tudor Howell, and Dr. Woodrow seemed to be the only people in the county who respected Jim Casey. And old Shipley at the Farmers State Bank. And maybe the county board of commissioners. Were it not for the taxes paid by the C Bar Cattle Co., the county would have to tax the living hell out of everyone else. The population of Oak County ought to respect Jim Casey. Instead most of the damned county had dirtied on him.

And Sheriff Jackson had to admit, when he thought about it, that the main reason he wanted to catch Jim Casey wasn't because the man was a fugitive from justice. Hell, there were hundreds, maybe even thousands, of fugitives in the western territories. No, it was a matter of pride now. Jim Casey had escaped from his jail. Escaped from him.

He'd fed his horse in a corral behind his three-room frame house and was walking to his office when he saw the young woman coming. Somehow just the sight of her boosted his spirits a notch. Her dad was a fraud, a quack and a con man, but he'd left now and she'd stayed. She was working for Dr. Woodrow and living at Mrs. Spencer's boarding house. Just seeing her on the streets of Rockledge was always a pleasure.

"Howdy, Miss Abraham." The sheriff tipped his hat.

"Hello, sheriff. Can I have a word with you?"

"Sure can, miss. Anytime."

"In your office?"

"You betcha." He led the way. His deputy was out somewhere. "Sit down there, Miss Abraham. Got something to talk about?"

She sat with her knees together and her hands in her lap, fingers twitching nervously. "What I would like to know . . . well, let me start over. I personally am not acquainted with Mr. Casey and I am not very familiar with the crime that he was convicted of. But I understand that testimony from a Mrs. Agnes Mooreman was damaging to his defense." She wasn't sure herself exactly what she wanted to say, and she paused.

"That's right. Her testimony sure didn't help Jim Casey."

"Well, as you know, as the whole town knows, we,

Dr. Woodrow operated on Mrs. Mooreman just yesterday. Dr. Woodrow thinks she will recover, and . . ." Ruth Ann's fingers were still twitching. She was trying to tactfully lead up to what she wanted to say, but she could think of no way to do it. Finally, she spoke bluntly. "I believe, from what she said before the surgery, that she and the Reverend Weems were intimate, and I believe she lied on the witness stand."

"Huh?" Sheriff Jackson was flabbergasted. "No. Not the reverend. Naw, couldn't be. What makes you say a thing like that?"

"She was afraid she was going to die, and she told me about going to church and confessing to her God, and she sort of made a confession to me."

"She said she lied?"

"Not exactly. What she said is—I'm trying to remember her exact words—she said that what she and the reverend did was no sin. She said they prayed together before and after. And she said she couldn't remember what words were spoken between the reverend and Mr. Casey, only that Mr. Casey was angry and carried a gun."

Sheriff Jackson's round, red face was a shade redder now. "What they did together? They prayed before and after? What did she mean?"

"Can't you guess? They were both single, and Mrs. Mooreman is an attractive woman."

"Oh." It came to him then. "Why, that's hard to believe."

"Perhaps if you think about it, it won't be so hard to believe. And I've heard rumors—just rumors, mind you—that the Reverend Weems showed an interest in other women."

"Oh no." The sheriff shook his head. "No, I can't believe that."

"How well did you know the reverend?"

"I, myself, didn't know him a-tall, but my wife, she went to his church, and the way she tells it you'd think he could've walked on water."

Ruth Ann stood. "I'm not sure I should be telling you what a patient told me. But considering everything, I just thought you, somebody, ought to know. A man was convicted of murder, and he could have been hung, might be yet, and one of the witnesses against him isn't sure that what she said in court is the truth."

"Jim Casey wouldn't have been hung. Judge Buckley ain't a hangin' judge. I've heard that from other law officers. He'd probably have sentenced Casey to twenty-five years in the pen."

"That's half a lifetime, and it would be ruinous to most men. Anyway, I thought you ought to know. It's possible the reverend wasn't, uh, without sin."

"Well . . . well . . ." Sheriff Jackson was still shaking his head in disbelief.

Chapter Fifteen

Her next stop was at the Doty house. The boy, Horace, was lying on a bed in the two-room shack built of a combination of logs and rough-sawn lumber. Mrs. Doty was washing clothes on a scrub board in a tub of soapy water. "Go on in and see 'im," she said, wringing out a pair of denim overalls.

"Hello, Horace. How are you today?"

Mrs. Doty followed her in, wiping her red, rough hands on an apron made of a flour sack. "His throat's too sore to talk."

"Has he been eating at all? Or drinking milk?"

"I got some milk down 'im, and I mixed some bread with the milk. Good thing we got a cow."

Ruth Ann sat on the edge of the bed. "Can you open your mouth for me, Horace?"

"He's been whinin' some."

"Mrs. Doty, do you have a lamp that you could bring over here? I need a better light."

"I'll fetch one."

While the mother was out of the room, Ruth Ann whispered, "You're a brave boy, Horace. You're a little man." From the small leather bag she carried, she removed a short, narrow clinical thermometer. "Let's take

111

your temperature. Let's put this under your tongue, and please don't bite it. It's only glass you know."

The boy did as asked. Ruth Ann used a railroad watch and her fingertips to count his pulse.

When the mother came back with a lamp, she removed the thermometer, frowned at it. "Open wide, Horace. That's a good boy. Hmm. It's healing, but it's still sore, isn't it, Horace." To Mrs. Doty, Ruth Ann said, "I need some warm water. Not hot, but warm. In a cup. Do you have any of the carbolic soap and laudanum left?"

"Yeah, we got some. My husband hurt his arm at work and he took some of the laudanum. I'll fetch some water."

Whispering again, Ruth Ann said, "I know it's sore. But you have to drink milk, Horace, and swallow some bread. It will get better, but you have to be strong. Eat as much as you can and it will get better. I promise. Will you do that?"

The boy nodded.

She swabbed his throat with carbolic soap and warm water. "Tastes awful, doesn't it Horace." Then she gave him a drink of bromide to help him sleep. "I'll be back tomorrow, Horace. Remember, eat as much as you can."

In the next room, out of the boy's earshot, she said, "His temperature is a little too high, and his pulse is not as strong as I wish it was. Try to get him to eat something soft. Oatmeal is good food. Do you have any oatmeal?"

"We ain't got much of anything. My husband don't get paid enough. I wish we had the farm back."

"Why did you leave the farm?"

"Couldn't grow nothin'. Couldn't grow much in the best years, and the last two years was so dry we couldn't grow nothin'."

"I see. So you sold the farm and moved to town?"

"Humph." The woman was bitter again. "Almost gave it away to that rich man, Mr. Casey. He gave us only half of what it was worth."

"I see. Hmm. Tell me, it's none of my business, but did you have to sell?"

"Couldn't grow nothin'. Had to leave."

Ruth Ann absorbed that, then asked, "What would you have done if Mr. Casey hadn't bought it?"

"Couldn't stay. But we stayed long enough to prove up on it and he shoulda paid more."

"Then, if Mr. Casey hadn't bought it you would have had to leave there with nothing, is that it?"

"He's rich. He shoulda paid more."

As soon as she checked with the doctor to see whether she was needed, Ruth Ann filled a burlap bag a quarter full of potatoes and carrots and walked to the Howell Mercantile where she bought a two-pound bag of rolled oats. Back at the Doty house, she waved away Mrs. Doty's thanks, then went to her room at the boardinghouse.

It was a good twelve miles between the Indian Creek camp and the Hatchet Lake camp. The horses hadn't completely recovered from the hard work the day before and they were happy to be off-saddled at Hatchet Lake and turned out to graze. Before turning them out, Levi roped another horse out of the grazing remuda to keep up at night.

Levi stayed on his horse to rope another. He didn't whirl the loop over his head, which would have caused the horses to move away from him. Instead, he brought the loop back, then up and over, giving his wrist a half-twist. The loop turned over in the air and settled around the head of the horse he wanted. Casey grinned. It was always a pleasure to watch old Levi with a catch rope.

Not only were their two mounts happy to be off-saddled, Casey and his hired man were glad to see the cabin was undisturbed and groceries were plentiful. Still, it was nearly noon, and the sheriff could be on his way up there from town.

Casey opened a hermetically sealed can of dried beef and another of red beans and carried them out to the trees where he'd left his bedroll. While he ate, he kept watch on the Glacier Trail, ready to hide if he saw anyone coming. No one came. Right after dark, Levi fried some meat and made a batch of biscuits. The two men had a good meal of steak, biscuits, and sorghum, topped off with dried fruit stewed to a softness.

Casey ate hastily, listening, fearful of hearing a man "Halloo the House." Meal over, he went to his bed under the pines. Levi quickly washed the dishes, leaving no clue as to how many men had been in the cabin.

At daylight, stomachs full, mounted on fresh horses, the two men began combing the hillsides and narrow valleys for cattle. "Gather all the dry stuff you see," Casey said. "I'd like to leave the mother cows." By midafternoon they had about fifty head. Levi held them in a bunch in a small treeless park while Casey cut out the cows with calves, then they started driving the herd south, toward Indian Creek.

Separating the cattle, driving them in a bunch, was a job that normally required at least four experienced cowboys, but the two men managed. At times they had to spur their horses into a dead run to head off cattle that wanted to leave, and at times they rode at a slow walk, trying not to excite the herd. For the hundredth time Casey was glad he'd hired old Levi. The old man

114

was the only cowboy Casey knew who could hold a bunch of half-wild longhorn cattle together by himself.

But Indian Creek was a long way to drive a herd of cattle, and just before dark, they left the herd and went back to Hatchet Lake. Before riding within sight of the cabin, Levi went ahead and scouted the place. Then he signaled his employer.

Next morning they were riding again on different horses. This time they carried two blankets apiece and some groceries in saddlebags. They rounded up the herd they'd abandoned the night before and got it moving. Along the way they picked up fifteen more yearlings and a few cows.

At dusk they were within sight of the Indian Creek cabin, and again Levi went ahead to be sure they were alone. When he came back, Casey said, "I'd like to get these brutes started downhill before it gets plumb dark. Think we can do it?"

"We can try like a steer."

They ate a cold meal in the unlighted cabin, and Casey joked, "I've read about people who were trying to lose weight. They ought to live the way we're living."

"I've never seen the day I couldn't use a few more pounds," Levi said, "but I've lived a lot worse than this and didn't get any skinnier."

In the morning, Casey made a decision. "We need horses. We can't ride these two to death. We're gonna have to go back to Hatchet Lake and bring eight or ten horses over here."

"If we hit a trot we can get there and back in a day."

"That's what we'll have to do. I hate to lose a day, but if we don't change horses once in a while we're gonna be afoot."

That's what it took, a full day. They brought a lantern

with them this time, and they put the stove back together and cooked a meal. "Those ponies we brought with us are grazing close in," Casey allowed, "and they'll drown out any sound of riders coming. I'm going to swallow now and chew later and get out of here."

"Ain't likely any lawdog is gonna ride up here in the dark, but I wouldn't gamble much on it."

Grinning, Casey allowed, "The odds are on my side, but I've got nothing to win and everything to lose. I apologize for leaving the dirty dishes for you to wash."

"See you mañana."

They spent the next day gathering the cattle they'd taken away from the three rustlers, and they rounded up about twenty-five more. At the end of the day, Casey said, "I'd guess about a hundred head altogether. What would you guess, Levi."

"Hunnerd and two."

Chuckling, Casey said, "You've been keeping count, huh?"

"That's how many we've had here over the past few days. How many we can get together in the mornin' is another horse's color."

"We've got all two men can handle. Maybe more."

"Shore glad we've got some fresh horses to start down that trail."

"I wish we could take a change of horses with us, but that would be almost impossible."

"Yup. Try to drive a few horses with a bunch of cattle, and them ol' ponies'd be down on the prairie and out of the territory before we got a good start."

"There's a good stout bay named Soogan that's the best bet. His shoes are getting a little thin, though. I hope there's enough daylight left that I can get him shod."

"I know 'im, and he's a good 'un. I'll set my saddle

on that blue roan. He likes to pitch a little early of a mornin', but he's tougher'n a boiled owl."

Grateful that the thieves had left some horseshoes and shoeing tools, Casey ran in the horses, caught the bay, and ninety minutes later had him standing on new iron. Levi kept watch. He allowed the roan's shoes were good enough.

By first light next morning they were back at work, and by midmorning they had about a hundred cattle gathered and started downhill. Then they rode back to the camp and switched their saddles to the two horses they would ride for the next several days. Blanket rolls tied behind the cantles and saddle pockets stuffed with groceries, they began the long cattle drive down out of the mountains.

They hadn't gone far when Levi saw two riders coming.

"Aw shit," Levi said. "Must be that damned sheriff."

The cattle were beginning to string out, but still were mostly in a bunch. Levi was on one side of the bunch and Casey was on the other side. Some of the cows had lost sight of their calves and were bawling.

Levi yelled to get Casey's attention, then pointed down the trail and held up two fingers. From where he was, Casey couldn't see the riders, but he knew what Levi was telling him. He swore, "Hell of a time for them to show up. Goddam, they could just . . . aw damn it to hell anyway." He reined his horse up into the timber and got behind a boulder out of sight.

What kind of lie could Levi tell them? They wouldn't believe he was working alone. No, they'd know Casey was near, and they'd hang around all day and maybe all night. Goddam it all. Shit. Goddam. Excuse me, Boots.

He dismounted, took off his hat, and peered over the top of the boulder. He watched the two riders come, scattering cattle out of their way. Sonsofbitches. Don't they know how much work it takes to gather that many cattle in this rough country? That goddam sheriff and his shit-for-brains deputy just didn't give a good goddam.

Then Casey breathed a sigh of relief. The riders were close enough now that he could see they were not Sheriff Jackson and his deputy. They were no one Casey had ever seen before.

But they were gunmen. Both hardcases. Up to no good.

Levi reined up and sat his saddle, watching them come. When they were close enough, the short, husky one said, "Howdy."

"Howdy."

"You handling these cattle by yourself?"

"Yup."

The other one, a mean-looking jasper with a thin face and a handlebar moustache, said, "That's gotta be hard to do."

"Ain't in no hurry."

The two turned in their saddles and studied the country around them, looking for more men. Casey ducked. Levi studied them. They were trouble.

"Where you gents headed?" he asked.

"Up yonder. Hear there's gold for the diggin'."

That was a lie. Levi knew where they were headed. The Indian Creek camp. They hadn't heard that the camp had already been ransacked and the horses stolen. How many thieves knew about the C Bar's troubles, anyway?

Casey was thinking the same thing. They weren't just drifting through. The Indian Creek Trail was first discovered by the Ute Indians, and later by the prospectors. But it went as far as the headwaters of Indian Creek and no farther. These men were looking for a chance to steal from the C Bar. Worse, if they thought Levi was alone they might kill him and take what cattle they thought they could handle. Or they might go on up to the camp and take the eight horses there.

Levi could outdraw and outshoot either one of the two, but not both. Casey had to do something. Shoot from here and shoot to kill? He'd still rather not kill anybody. No, best thing to do was disarm them. Take their guns away and they'd be no threat.

Drawing the Navy Colt, Casey took aim. Try to put a slug past that short jasper's left ear, he said to himself. Make them look this way. All right, Levi, get ready.

Casey squinted down the short barrel and squeezed the trigger.

Chapter Sixteen

The two riders jerked their heads in the direction the shot had come from, eyes wide, hands going to their guns.

Levi barked, "Don't move."

When they looked back at him they were looking at the bore of his big Army Colt.

"Keep your hands away from them guns," he said. "Stay right still and we might let you live."

White-faced, the short one said, "Wha ... what're you pointin' guns at us for?"

"We don't like your looks."

"We ... we ain't done nothin' to you."

"And you ain't goin' to neither."

"How many of you are there?"

"Enough to blow you out of your saddles. Just set right still and keep your hands where I can see 'em."

Casey saw that Levi had them covered, and he left the boulder and led his horse to them, gun in hand, hammer back, ready to shoot again. Without a word, he went to the right side of each rider and took their six-guns. Then he said, "Get down."

They dismounted, eyes wary, a little fearful. The short one asked, "What're you gonna do? We ain't done nothin'."

Casey answered, "We mean you no harm, but we've been stolen from so much we can't trust anybody." To Levi, he said, "What do you think we should do with them?"

Instead of answering, Levi asked the short one, "How'd you know the C Bar is shorthanded? In Denver?"

"We don't know nothin' about no C Bar."

"The hell, you beller. You didn't come up here to look for gold. You wouldn't find any if you did. You heard about a cow camp up here with some good horses and no men. Where'd you hear about it?"

The other man spoke, "If I tell you will you let us go?"

"We won't kill you," Casey answered.

"Yeah, we heard about it in Denver. What we heard is the C Bar is the biggest cow outfit in the territory, and all the men done quit 'cause the boss is on the run from the law and can't pay 'em. We heard about a cow camp up here."

"Who told you?"

"Some jasper that said he usta work for the C Bar."

"What's his name?"

"I don't know, and that's a fact."

"What's he look like?"

The man shrugged. "Like ever'body else. Said he quit the C Bar 'bout a year ago and was in Rockledge when the boss broke out of jail. Said he talked to a couple of cowhands that just rode down from the camp."

"Where were you planning to sell the horses?"

"We wasn't plannin' to steal no horses."

"You're lying. Is there a market in Denver?"

"Don't know, and that's a fact."

Casey considered that, then said, "I know you're lying, and I know you had stealing on your minds. For that reason, we'll keep your guns."

"You can't do that. That's agin the law."

Levi said, "I'll bet a dollar you're wanted by the law somewheres. Go ahead and tell the laws all about us, then answer their questions about yourselfs."

"Just go back to Denver. Go on ahead of us. We don't want you shooting us in the back."

"Wait a minute," Levi said. "Watch 'em, Jim." He dismounted and searched the men's saddlebags for more guns, then searched the men. "Now you can git."

It took three days to drive a hundred cattle down the Indian Creek Trail to the prairie east of Colorado's front range. They had to move cattle through thick willow bushes, buck brush, and timber and around boulders. One day they moved only about five miles.

Sitting close to a small fire that night, eating bacon broiled on a stick, Levi said, "I been up to that goddam Denver. It's the asshole of the world. There's men in Denver that'd cut your throat for a quarter. A lot of cowboys hang around town, some lookin' for work and some that don't wanta work. If somebody from Rockledge went up there and said somethin' about the troubles we're havin', half of them fellers'd be down here stealin' ever'thing they could drive away. Or pack away."

"I'm afraid that's what's happened. I remember a man who quit about a year ago. I heard he hired out to some mining company as a shotgun guard. I'll bet he's the one who spread the word."

"I re'clect him. Art, was his name. He was a bellyacher, and nobody was unhappy when he quit."

"Yep, he had a drink at Rockledge with Buzz and

122

Arnold, then quit the mining company and went to Denver."

They rolled up in their blankets, and at first light began another day. They drove the cattle down to an abandoned homestead on the prairie, then stopped.

"As good a place as any," Casey allowed.

"Can't go no further anyhow," Levi said. "Horses give out, our stomachs growlin'."

They were on C Bar land, but about fifteen miles from the ranch headquarters, halfway between headquarters and the company's Squaw Mountain camp. The man and wife Casey had hired to hold down the permanent camp didn't seem too stable, and Levi reckoned they'd pulled out. So after talking it over they decided that Levi would ride to headquarters and bring back more groceries and as many horses as he could lead.

If the thieves hadn't been there and taken everything.

Casey would try to keep the herd from scattering too far, but he knew that was hopeless. His horse was too weary, and he was too hungry to do much work. He'd unroll his blankets somewhere near the old homestead shack, eat what dried beef they had left. And wait.

Mrs. Carter saw four men coming. She'd been expecting unwanted visitors, and she kept the doors and windows of the house locked. And she kept Mr. Casey's Winchester repeating rifle loaded and handy.

They came from the north, two in a light wagon pulled by two horses, and two on horseback. They stopped just out of rifle range and looked the place over. Then the two on horseback rode forward cautiously, heads swiveling to take in everything.

Mrs. Carter had carried everything from the barn that looked valuable, two saddles and harness for four horses. It was all piled on the floor of the main room next to the rock fireplace. Everything that was worth stealing and could be carried away was in the house. She watched through a window in an upstairs bedroom.

The two on horseback waved to the two in the wagon, and soon all four were gathered in front of the barn. They went first into the bunkhouse and came out empty handed. Then the barn. They looked to the house.

Mrs. Carter opened a window just enough to poke the rifle barrel through and squint down the barrel. She placed a box of .44-40 shells on the floor beside her and cocked the hammer back. When two of the men started walking toward the house she fired.

The exploding cartridge sounded like a cannon in the room. The two men stopped dead still, trying to see where the shot had come from. They talked, half-turned, and yelled something at the other men. Mrs. Carter levered in another shell and fired again. She saw the lead slug kick up dirt between the two.

They wheeled and ran, ducked behind the wagon. They stayed there a while with only the tops of their hats showing. Mrs. Carter had had no experience with thieves but she knew what they were talking about. They were trying to figure out how many men were in the house, and if only one, how to shoot that one without getting shot. They'd come here from somewhere north to loot the place, and they wouldn't give up easily.

Lord, she wished Mrs. Casey were here. Mrs. Casey had fought thieves and rustlers and Indians. She'd put the fear of God into these four right fast. Alone, Mrs. Carter knew she couldn't do it. She could only watch one side of the house at a time. Soon the four would realize they had only one shooter to deal with, and they'd come in the back doors and windows. Smash them open. She should have shot to kill instead of to scare, but she'd never as much as pointed a gun at a human before. Killing was just not her nature. But she had to do it. Kill them or they'd kill her.

Almost inaudibly, Mrs. Carter recited the Lord's Prayer and aimed the Winchester.

The sodbuster family had left nothing at all when they'd moved out of the two-room shack. Glass was broken out of the windows, the roof was ready to collapse, floorboards were broken. The door hung open on one hinge. As soon as Casey stepped through the door a gray packrat ran across the room and disappeared under a broken floorboard.

In a storm, the shack would be better than nothing, but a man would have to be desperate to try to live in it.

Outside again, he looked over a hundred and sixty acres of Russion thistles, bind weeds, and high yellow clover. Worthless. Casey shook his head sadly. What was once good grass land was now nothing. Land that had been plowed and abandoned was never the same. A man couldn't even ride a horse across it without getting the horse tangled in the wire fences left behind, wire that was hidden in the weeds. Casey had hoped, when he bought the land, that one day he could plow it again and plant wild grass, something that would grow in a semiarid climate, something that would feed cattle. But as yet, he'd done nothing with it.

That preacher, that rabble-rousing Reverend Weems, had called him a land grabber. Even called him a land thief. At least he wasn't a land waster. And he'd paid for it. The U.S. Congress decided that land open for homesteading for five years and still unclaimed could be bought for $1.25 an acre. Jim and Boots Casey had bought all the land they could. To do it, they'd suffered, trying to keep warm in the winter in a dirt-floor shack, working dawn to dark every day of the year to keep their cows on the best grazing land in the territory and to keep their cows from dying while calving. They'd been half-frozen saving their cattle in blizzards. They'd lived on wild meat instead of eating their own beef. They'd fought off rustlers and marauding Indians.

So he'd paid only seventy-five cents an acre for the abandoned homesteads. So he'd refused to allow farmers to dam the creeks and draw irrigation water from them. Dammit, he and Boots were here first. They'd bought the land along the creeks, knowing they had to control the water. That damned preacher couldn't expect them to stand around with their hands in their pockets and let the farmers dam the creeks while their cattle died of dehydration.

Thinking about it, Casey muttered, "Call us land grabbers and thieves, huh. Shit. Excuse me, Boots."

A lead bullet from a rim-fire cartridge, fired by a Winchester repeating rifle, knocked splinters off the top edge of the wagon box only inches from a man's head. The man ducked out of sight. While Mrs. Carter levered in another cartridge two bullets came through the window, smashing glass and slamming into the far wall. Another thudded into the side of the house near the window. Instinctively, Mrs. Carter ducked.

Two men ran from behind the wagon into the barn.

For a long moment after that it was quiet. Finally, Mrs. Carter summoned her courage and peered over the windowsill. Two hats showed behind the wagon. With fear in her heart, she knew the other two had gone out the other end of the barn and were circling to get behind the house.

She had to keep shooting, couldn't just stay under the window and cover up her head. She put the rifle barrel through the window, aimed, and fired at a pair of boots now visible under the wagon. She fired again, then ducked and shoved short, blunt cartridges into the loading gate on the side of the Winchester.

The latch on the kitchen door was splintered with a sickening crash. The door slammed open. Boots pounded the kitchen floor.

Mrs. Carter left the bedroom and went to the head of the stairs. A man appeared at the bottom. She shot from the hip, levered in another cartridge, and shot again.

Half-crying, Mrs. Carter fired, levered, fired, levered, fired. At the same time, while tears ran down her cheeks, she mumbled:

"Yea, though I walk through the valley of death . . ."

Chapter Seventeen

Levi was about a mile from headquarters when he heard the shooting. "Oh, gawd, no," he muttered, spurring his tired horse into a lope. "Sorry, feller. Mrs. Carter is there alone."

While he rode he checked the loads in his Army Colt. How many thieves were trying to take the house away from her? How long could she hold them off? Not long. "Keep them legs goin', feller."

He rode into the ranch yard in time to see two men running toward the front door with guns in their hands. He could hear shooting inside the house. He snapped a shot to stop them, then dropped off his horse and let the horse go on by. Flat on his belly in the open yard, he heard a slug hit the ground near his head, ignored it, aimed the Colt with both hands and fired.

A man dropped. The other ran around a corner of the house.

Immediately, Levi was up and running, running as fast as his seventy-five-year-old legs could carry him. He hit the front door with his left shoulder. Didn't budge it. Wheeling, he ran off the front porch and around to the kitchen door. It was open. Guns were still booming inside. She was still alive. But there were men in the house shooting at her. Seconds counted.

Without thinking of his own safety, Levi ran through the kitchen, holding his six-gun straight out at eye level. He spotted a man at the foot of the stairs. His gun popped. The man spun around and fell. Another gun opened up, and a bullet splintered the frame of the kitchen door. Out of the corner of his eyes, Levi saw the shooter, wheeled, and fired three rapid shots, fanning the hammer.

The shots were too rapid, too hasty, and he missed. But the man didn't shoot again. Instead he ran from that room around a corner and into the main room. Levi heard the bolt latch jerked back, heard the front door yanked open, heard boots running across the porch.

Levi yelled, "Mrs. Carter. Mrs. Carter, it's me, Levi. Don't shoot."

Cautiously, he went to the foot of the stairs, looked up at her. She was sitting on her feet at the top, rifle in her hands. Tears were running down her face.

Taking the stairs two at a time, Levi felt the age in his knees, but didn't let it slow him. At her side, he said, "Mrs. Carter, are you hurt?"

Through tear-filled eyes she looked up at him. "No, Levi. I don't think so. Thank God you're here."

"How many are there?"

"Four. That's all I saw."

"Two're down. The others ran. They won't be back."

"Did I . . . did I kill anybody?"

"No. I did." He sat beside her, put an arm around her, and let her cry on his shoulder.

"Thank God," she mumbled.

"You didn't kill anybody, but you held 'em off. You're a brave woman, Mrs. Carter. I'm proud to know you."

It took some arguing to get Mrs. Carter to go to town. "My boss, Mrs. Casey, wouldn't leave," she said. "Mrs. Casey would stay here and fight the whole Union army. Mrs. Casey was good to me, and I can't leave her things here for the stealers. Rest her soul."

Levi explained that Jim Casey was waiting at an abandoned homesteader's shack and needed chuck and fresh horses. "Somebody has to go to town and fetch the sheriff. Them thieves left a team and wagon here. You can drive that to town. Let the sheriff pick up the corpses."

"All right," she said reluctantly. "Somebody has to fetch the sheriff. But I'm comin' back."

"I'll catch another horse and ride partway with you to make sure them two don't show up again. Then I got to get back to Jim."

The team and light wagon came down First Street at a trot, driven by an overweight woman with a harried look on her face. Ruth Ann watched as the woman whoaed the team in front of the sheriff's office, climbed down from the wagon, and dropped the driving lines onto the street. The door to the sheriff's office was locked.

"Ma'am," the woman said, obviously terribly upset about something, "do you know where I can find the sheriff?"

"Why," Ruth Ann answered, "I believe the deputy is in the cafe. I'll go get him if you want."

"I'd sure appreciate it. Hurry, will you please?"

Deputy Rankin was sitting at the counter, sipping coffee. It was late afternoon, but too early for supper. Ruth Ann marched right up to him.

"Deputy Rankin, there's a woman at your office who

needs to see you or the sheriff. Can you come? She seems to be terribly upset."

Gulping a mouthful, the deputy looked up at Ruth Ann. "Aw, can't a man finish his coffee?"

"Something's happened. I don't know what."

"Aw, dangit. Wish Walt would stay in town more, steda tryin' to catch that jail breaker." He wiped his mouth with the back of his hand and stood.

Ruth Ann's curiosity couldn't be controlled. She hurried, right behind the deputy, and got to his office in time to hear the woman blurt, ". . . men are dead they came to steal from the house and I shot at them and then Levi came and shot two of them and the other two ran. Please come and do something."

"Calm down, now Missuz, uh, what's your name?"

"I'm Mrs. Carter and I'm cook and housekeeper at the ranch, and . . ."

"You say you was there alone when some looters came, but Levi came along in time to help you?"

"Yessir. I shot at them but I didn't hit anybody and Levi shot two of them."

"Where is Levi?"

"He just came down from one of the cow camps, and he needed some groceries and some more horses, and he said he had to get back to the camp but he'll come back to the ranch tomorrow."

A small crowd had gathered by now, all listening intently. Deputy Rankin glanced at them, then said, "All right. The sheriff is off somewhere tryin' to track down your boss. I'll go in your wagon. The team don't look too tired." He offered a helping hand to Mrs. Carter, got her seated on the spring wagon seat, then picked up the driving lines and climbed up himself. To one of the townsmen he said, "Tell Walt where I'm at." He clucked to the team, turned the rig around in the street.

The townsman, a lean-jawed middle-aged gent, turned faded eyes to Ruth Ann. "Did you hear what all she said? Somethin' 'bout a shootin' at the C Bar?"

"I gathered," Ruth Ann said to the handful of men, women, and kids, "that the woman, Mrs. Carter, was at the ranch alone when some men came to steal, to loot the place. She shot at them, and then Mr. Levi came along and shot two of them."

An elderly man with no teeth cackled. "By durn, ain't been so much goin' on around here since this town was bornded."

Ruth Ann got back to the clinic in time to see Dr. Woodrow finish cutting a plaster cast off the wrist of a young dark-haired woman. The woman was very pretty in spite of two overlapping front teeth which showed when she smiled. And she was smiling.

Sitting on the doctor's examination table, her legs dangling over the side, she said, "This scar on my lip, Doctor, will it ever heal?"

Dr. Woodrow took a closer look at her face, putting his face close to hers. She looked into his eyes and continued a slow smile.

"Yes," he said. "It won't be long now. A few weeks from now it won't show at all."

"Thank goodness. I wouldn't want to be disfigured." Her smile was meant to be tantalizing. For a few seconds, Ruth Ann felt a hint of jealousy. But the doctor was strictly professional.

"You won't be disfigured, Mrs. Rankin, I promise you that."

"I surely appreciate your attention, Doctor." Her voice was syrupy sweet, Ruth Ann thought.

"The bones in your wrist appears to be completely regenerated, but don't put much stress on it yet. Give it at least three more weeks before you do any heavy lifting with it."

"I'll do whatever you say, doctor."

Ugh, thought Ruth Ann, but she made no sound. Instead, she busied herself, putting the doctor's razor-sharp shears back in the instrument cabinet, picking up the discarded plaster cast, pretending to ignore the conversation.

But when the dark-haired woman left, she had to ask, "You called her Mrs. Rankin. Is she related to the deputy sheriff?"

"His wife."

"Oh? She's very pretty. How did she fracture her wrist?"

"She said she tripped and fell. It happens. She put her hands out to break the fall and suffered a simple fracture of the left wrist."

"And the scar on her upper lip?"

Smiling, the doctor said, "Why do you ask?"

"Oh." Ruth Ann tried to fake disinterest by shrugging. "You know me. I'm full of questions."

"For your information, Miss Busybody, she didn't completely break the fall and her face collided with the floor." Dr. Woodrow was smiling when he said that. "How is the Doty boy?"

"He's healing, but he's pale and weak. I'm afraid he's not eating enough."

"Perhaps I should go see him."

"I wish you would. I've been telling him and his mother that he should eat more. You're more authoritative. Perhaps they will carry out your orders."

"And Mrs. Mooreman?"

"Healing slowly. It looks to me like it will be a while yet before the sutures can come out, but I'm not the doctor."

133

"Her bowel movements?"

"Normal, she says. Only a slight pain now and then. Fortunately, she always has friends present to attend to her needs and to cook soup for her. Because of them I don't have to deal with the bed pan."

"Well, I'll drop in on her, too. First thing in the morning."

Ruth Ann offered for the third or fourth time to cook supper for the doctor, but as always he declined, saying it wouldn't look right. "I don't pay much attention to what goes on in Rockledge," he said, "but I do know that rumors run rampant."

"That's true in any small town." Ruth Ann smiled wryly. "Especially the juicy kind, like the relationship between a doctor and his woman assistant."

"Yes. We don't want to give them as much as a hint of impropriety."

"No-o-o," Ruth Ann said with a hint of sarcasm. "That wouldn't do at all."

Chapter Eighteen

What to do? Levi wanted to be at headquarters when the sheriff came, and he also wanted to get some chuck to Jim Casey as soon as possible. If he wasn't there when the sheriff arrived, he'd have some explaining to do, and he wasn't a very good liar. He'd have to wait, that's all there was to it. He had some things to do before he headed back south anyway. Jim had gone hungry before, and he wouldn't starve.

Levi didn't touch the dead men, only bent over them to be sure they were dead. Looking at the jagged line of mountains to the west, he figured he had only an hour of daylight left. The sheriff was going to have to do whatever he wanted to do in the dark. Levi ran in the horses, picked out four, and turned the others out again. He saddled one and put halters with lead ropes on the others.

With tools from a storage shed, he fixed the latch on the kitchen door, then built a fire in the cookstove. At dusk he lighted some lamps and lanterns. Then he mixed some pancake batter, fried fourteen pancakes on the big griddle and some cured ham. He ate four of the pancakes and some of the ham, then wrapped the rest in wax paper.

Going through the cabinets, he got more groceries together, including apple butter, a slab of bacon that looked like it wouldn't spoil for a few days, some dried apples, and canned fruit. He brought in his saddlebags and stuffed them full. Upstairs, he found another rifle. This one had a longer barrel than the Winchester and a trap door for loading a single metallic cartridge at a time. A hunting rifle. It was in a saddle boot specially made for it. Leaving the Winchester for Mrs. Carter, he carried the long-barreled gun and a handful of cartridges outside and strapped the boot to the left side of his saddle.

By then it was dark. Lighting two lanterns, he hung one on the front porch, the other at the entrance to the barn. It occurred to him that for the second time his boss, Jim Casey, was depending on him to fetch chuck, and for the second time he was being delayed.

Sorry, Jim, he said under his breath. Things just ain't turnin' out right.

When he heard the wagon coming, trace chains rattling, wheels creaking, he carried a lantern out to meet it. Somehow, seeing Deputy Rankin with Mrs. Carter instead of the sheriff disappointed him. The deputy wasn't quite the professional the sheriff was. He led him to the body in the ranch yard, held the lantern close while the deputy looked over the body, then led him into the house.

"How'd they get in?" the deputy asked.

"Broke in the kitchen door."

"It don't look busted."

"I just fixed it."

"You shouldn't have done that. You're not s'posed to touch anything until an officer of the law examines it."

"It ain't as good as new. You can see it was busted."

"You shouldn't have done it."

136

Locking eyes with the deputy, Levi said flatly, "It needed fixin' and I fixed it."

"The sheriff ain't gonna like it."

Levi stayed in the kitchen, but Mrs. Carter followed Deputy Rankin as he went through the house, noting the bullet holes in the floor and walls, the shattered window in the bedroom, and the empty .44-40 casings near the window and at the head of the stairs. Finally, the deputy said, "Well, whatever they came here for they didn't get it. Lost a team and wagon instead. I'll confiscate it, drive it back to town, and let the sheriff decide what to do with it. You," he said to Levi, "where was you when the shootin' started?"

"I was comin' down from . . ." Levi had started to say he was coming down from Hatchet Lake, but two questions popped into his mind: Where was Sheriff Jackson? Had he gone up to Hatchet Lake? He could have. If he'd gone up the Indian Creek trail they would have seen him. Thinking fast, he said, "Uhem, I was comin' from Indian Creek when I heard the gunfire."

Glancing at the packed saddlebags, the deputy said, "Looks like you're goin' back."

"Yup. That's where most of the C Bar stock is and I'm workin' for the C Bar 'till somebody tells me different."

The answer seemed to satisfy the deputy. "Help me load them bodies in the wagon. I think I can see that wagon road in the dark."

"You oughtta go back to town with 'im," Levi said to Mrs. Carter.

"I'm staying."

"You ain't scared?"

She hesitated a moment before she answered, "No."

"I wish I could stay here with you, but I can't."

"I'll stay."

The wagon no more than rattled out of the yard than Levi was in the corral, tying three horses head to tail. He rode south, leading the horses, hoping he could find the abandoned homestead by the light of a quarter moon.

Four riders were coming from the south. Jim Casey quickly saddled his horse and mounted. He couldn't outshoot four men, but if they saw him they'd know the cattle here weren't unguarded. It worked. The four stopped, looked his way for a long moment, then turned around and rode out of sight. They were strangers.

After dark, Casey built a small fire to guide Levi. He had nothing left to eat, but Levi should be back soon. Unless something went wrong. All kinds of things could go wrong. The sheriff might have detained Levi, or the old man might have run into a bunch of thieves. Aw hell, no use worrying about what might have happened. Wait and hope.

It was around midnight when he heard the old man holler, "Jim. It's me. I'm comin' in."

While Casey ate bacon wrapped in cold pancakes, Levi told him what had happened. Casey swore, "Sonsofbitches. I wish Mrs. Carter would go to town and stay there. It ain't safe for a woman alone. Hell, it ain't safe for a man alone."

Squatting on his heels, watching Casey eat, Levi allowed, "Well, they went there expectin' to steal a wagon load, but two of 'em are dead and they lost their team and wagon. Maybe they'll go back to Denver or wherever they come from and tell ever'body about it and maybe them hooligans'll figger stealin' from the C Bar ain't such a good idea."

Glumly, Casey said, "Maybe."

At sunup, they were traveling again, riding fresh horses and leading three others. Shortly after noon they were back at the Indian Creek Cowcamp, glad to see the place was the way they'd left it and horses grazing in the small pasture. They stayed only long enough to fry some bacon and eat the rest of the cold pancakes, then they were on their way north to the Hatchet Lake camp. Both believed they were more likely to find cattle close to the camp at Hatchet Lake, and it would be easier to round up a hundred head.

"If we can gather a hundred cattle around there, then we'll need about a hundred more," Casey said. "We should find that many around Squaw Mountain."

Levi grunted an agreement. But silently, both men were thinking the same thing: rustlers could get there first. Also on their minds was the fact that only a short time ago the C Bar employed eight men, and now there was only one. One hired man and the boss, trying to do a job that normally would take at least six men.

As before, the hired man rode up to the cabin alone in the dark. Casey hung back until he saw lamplight in the window and saw Levi's signal. "The sheriff's been here," Levi said. "He built hisself a fire and made hisself some coffee. That was just yesterday."

"Surely, he won't be back for a while."

"Prob'ly not, but he's a tricky sumbuck."

Cattle were scattered over so much steep rocky territory that they found only a few at a time. It took four days to round up a hundred head. Then two more days to drive them to the Indian Creek camp. A man on horseback could ride down the Indian Creek Trail to the abandoned homestead in about six hours, but it took four days for two men to move a hundred half-wild cattle down the trail. Four days of yelling, whistling, horses scrambling up the side of steep hills, pushing through dense willows and buck brush.

But finally they chased the last yearling out of an arroyo onto the prairie on the east side of the Front Range. Both men sat their saddles on horses that had gone almost as far as they could go. From there they could see the homestead and the country for miles around it. Their eyes, used to seeing long distances, scanned the country, the old shack, every clump of grass, every willow tree that grew along the creek. They looked at each other, jaws clamped tight. Levi's Adam's apple moved up and down his throat as he swallowed. He spoke softly, sadly:

"Not another cow brute in sight."

Jim Casey couldn't speak. His heart was in his stomach. It all seemed so hopeless. If he'd been a free man he might have been able to catch the rustlers before they got to the railroad loading pens at Castle Rock. He might have gotten some help from the officers of the law. But hell, if he went to the law he'd be arrested on sight. All he could do now was round up more cattle. Do it all over. He owned more than four thousand head of cattle, but rounding up and holding three hundred and fighting off rustlers was too big a job for two men. If he'd been free he could have hired more men. He had money in the bank to pay them. But he couldn't get to the bank. It was just hopeless.

All his life he'd worked and fought for everything he got. When things didn't go right, he'd just put his head down and worked harder, shot straighter. He and Boots. Now . . .

He'd never felt so frustrated in his life.

Chapter Nineteen

It had been a long night for Dr. Woodrow. Two bodies to examine. A paper to sign, spelling out the cause of death. Deputy Rankin helped him carry the bodies in and lay them out on the examination table, and Sheriff Waltham Jackson came along and helped strip the corpses and then dress them again after the examination. The only wounds were bullet wounds, which made the cause of death easy to determine. Wallets on the dead men showed both were from Denver. Sheriff Jackson grumbled that he'd have to send telegrams to the Denver police who, he hoped, would find some next of kin. There would be a coroner's inquest, and Mrs. Carter and Levi would have to testify. If he could find Levi.

It was near daylight before the bodies were taken away to a shed south of town near the unfenced cemetery.

Dr. Woodrow didn't even get to finish his breakfast before he had a patient. The man said he was "all bound up." The doctor prescribed some Calomel, a laxative made of mercurous chloride. The next patient was a small rancher who lived alone up north and who had a problem that was just the opposite. He'd eaten some meat that he shouldn't have. "I knew it didn't smell just right, but it was all the meat I had," he explained. "I been shittin' like a goose for three days now. I don't think I got any insides left."

The prescription was for a paregoric, a tincture of opium and camphor.

Net profit was ten dollars each for the autopsies and two dollars each from the patients. Not much, but half a month's pay for most men.

When Ruth Ann came in, Dr. Woodrow asked her to keep the clinic open and tell any visitors he'd be back soon. He packed his black leather satchel and went to visit his home-bound patients. While he was gone, Ruth Ann scrubbed the examination table, the floor, and kitchen, washed the breakfast dishes, peeled some potatoes and put them in cold water.

Her hands were red and rough from the work she was doing when Attorney Amos P. Sharp knocked on the door. She recognized him, but had no idea why he was there until he introduced himself and explained:

"I came to town to check with the sheriff, and he told me about a visit you had with him during which you expressed serious doubt as to the veracity of testimony given by Mrs. Agnes Mooreman."

"Oh yes. I suppose you should be told about it, but I hope the sheriff told no one else."

"I don't believe he did. May I sit?"

"Oh, I'm sorry, please do." Over coffee at the doctor's kitchen table, Ruth Ann told the lawyer the same thing she'd told the sheriff. Amos P. Sharp was pleased. He was also displeased.

"Her testimony was vague. She couldn't remember exactly what was said between the defendant and the Reverend Weems, but she insisted that what the defendant said was a threat. The jury believed her. Now she has admitted to you that she isn't sure."

He paused a moment, and Ruth Ann waited for him to go on.

"The problem is, what a patient says to a doctor or to a doctor's assistant is privileged. It is not acceptable in a court of law."

"Oh." Ruth Ann was disappointed. "I'm not knowledgeable about the law. So we have to persuade Mrs. Mooreman to repeat this to somebody else."

"Correct. If we could do that and get it on record, the judge might set aside the verdict and grant my motion for a new trial. That would be much quicker than arguing before the appellate court for a new trial."

While they talked, Dr. Woodrow returned and, after shaking hands, poured himself a cup of coffee and sat at the table with them. When the lawyer explained his hope and problem, the doctor frowned, first at Ruth Ann, then at the lawyer.

"As much as I would like to help Mr. Casey, I must protect my patients. I'm sorry, but Mrs. Mooreman is too weak at this time to answer questions."

"I can't question her without your permission, Doctor, but I would like very much to send to my home office for a stenographer and get a statement from her. It will take a steno a few days to arrive. Perhaps in the meantime, Mrs. Mooreman's condition will improve."

Ruth Ann said, "With a lawyer present, there's a chance she'll deny telling me anything."

"Ye-es." Amos P. Sharp pursed his lips as he thought it over. "It would help if you were there, Miss Abraham. And perhaps a personal friend of Mrs. Mooreman's."

"I'll be there if you need me."

* * *

"How is she doing?" Ruth Ann asked after the lawyer left.

"As well as can be expected." Dr. Woodrow spat out the words, and Ruth Ann knew he was irritated.

"Did I make a mistake by telling all this to the sheriff?"

"Yes, Ruth Ann, you did." The doctor's face was red. "It is extremely unethical for a doctor, or any medical personnel, to discuss what a patient says, or does, or is, with anyone."

"Whoops. I was afraid of that."

"Then why didn't you ask me?"

"I thought I was doing the right thing. I made a mistake."

"Do not ever do that again."

Now Ruth Ann's face was turning red. "I learned that a man's life is being ruined over a crime that he might not have committed. I had to tell somebody. I have ethics, too."

"I repeat, do not do that again."

Ruth Ann snapped back, "All right. I made a mistake. Why don't you just fire me?"

Suddenly, Dr. Woodrow's face went blank. He opened and closed his mouth without saying anything. He stammered, cleared his throat, and finally spoke again in a calm but barely audible voice:

"Will you marry me?"

"If I was you, Levi, I'd roll up my bed, saddle my private horse, and ride away from here. Forget the C Bar."

"Where would I go, Jim? I'm too old to hire on anywhere else."

"Didn't you save anything from your wages?"

"Yeah, I saved some, but unless I die young I ain't got enough to live on the rest of my life."

They sat cross-legged on the ground near the homesteader's shack. Their two horses were off-saddled and hobbled, resting and grazing.

"Huh," Casey snorted, "die young, you won't."

"Naw," Levi agreed, gazing across the prairie, "with my luck I'd run out of money in a few years and live to be a hunnerd."

"You stick around here and you'll work yourself to death or starve to death or get shot to death before you get a chance to spend what you've saved."

The old man lifted a hand, and Casey recognized that as a sign he'd discussed it long enough. Switching the subject, Levi asked, "How do they do it, Jim? Used to be a feller could drive off a big herd of cattle and shove 'em across the Rio Grande and pick up about fifty cents on the dollar. How do they change rustled cattle to cash around here?"

"Well," Casey leaned back on his elbows and stretched his legs, "up to now all I lost was a few head at a time. The thieves sold them one or two at a time to somebody who butchered them immediately. When you own around four thousand cattle, losing six or eight now and then doesn't seem like a big loss. But, as a feller said, you can be nickeled and dimed to death. And these homesteaders, they run low on chuck and they see all these cattle and they figure nobody will miss one, so they kill one to feed their families. You and I both have seen hides and heads on the ground where somebody—some town worker—shot and butchered a beef and carried away the meat. If you let them get by with it, you damned sure will be nickeled and dimed to death. You've heard all this before, and you've helped me catch a couple of nesters

145

in the act and report them to the sheriff. You know how that turned out."

"Yup. I know. The juries wouldn't convict 'em."

"These damned farmers believed what that preacher told them, that Boots and I are rich and we're—we were—picking on the poor."

"I re'clect, Jim, not long ago either, when you gave a beef to a family of six that was tryin' to scratch out a livin' down east of Squaw Mountain."

"There's a difference between giving it away and having it stolen from you. But in answer to your question, I'm not sure I know. Now that the railroad's built south from Denver, with shipping pens at Denver and Castle Rock, it only takes a few days to gather a bunch of cattle and ship them out of the state. A legitimate buyer won't touch them without having them looked over by a state brand inspector, but there are dishonest buyers. And bills of sale can be forged. I'd guess that's what's happened."

Levi leaned forward and put his elbows on his knees. "There's packin' houses that'll buy beefs with no questions asked if the price is right. But a hunnerd head might be more'n they could handle right fast."

"Yeah, and if an officer of the law asked questions, they might have a hard time explaining what happened to the hides with brands on them. But . . ." Casey shifted positions on the ground, "like the feller says, where there's a will there's a way."

After letting his horse rest a while, Levi resaddled and rode north. Casey was right when he suggested that one of them ought to check on Mrs. Carter and pick up some groceries, if any groceries were left. Levi would get there after dark, and he'd holler his head off to let Mrs. Carter know who was coming. That's what he did. He found everything at headquarters the way he'd left it, but the kitchen was getting low on food.

"I'll take what we've got to Jim in the mornin', then come back here and harness a team and go to town and buy some chuck myownself. I've got an account in the bank."

"I'll go with you. The sheriff told me to tell you he has to get statements in writing from us about the two men you shot."

"I reckon he has to do that. I wanta see 'im anyways about some rustled stock."

"Rustled stock? Oh my."

Levi told her about it. She sat at the kitchen table with her chin in her hands. "Poor Mr. Casey. The poor, poor man."

"He's lived through some tough times, him and his wife, but this's gotta be about the toughest time he's seen yet."

After a long silence, Levi drawled, "Right now I could use some coffee and anything to eat you can find."

"I'll find something."

Casey let his horse rest and graze overnight, then rode south in the morning to the C Bar's permanent camp at Squaw Mountain. His stomach complained, but he ignored it. Like the two off-breed camps, the Squaw Mountain camp was deserted. Not a cow or horse anywhere. The three-room clapboard house was empty. A broken child's wooden scooter lay in the front yard. That and a rag doll with no head, a few worn-out clothes, and a broken chair were all that was left behind by a family of four.

The team and wagon he'd furnished for the hired man's family was gone, too. Probably used by the family to move.

Casey swallowed a dry lump in his throat. His stomach grumbled. About two hundred head of cattle and, let's see, twenty, thirty, thirty-two horses gone. Stolen. And he couldn't go after them.

Shit. Excuse me, Boots.

Chapter Twenty

Amos P. Sharp was back with an elderly woman, whom he introduced as a secretary from his Denver law office. Dr. Woodrow went ahead of them to the home of Mrs. Agnes Mooreman. They waited outside while he went in. Eventually, he came out and advised them: "You can question her briefly. Not extensively. She is sitting up now, and a friend is with her. However, she said she does not wish to answer questions about the trial."

"If she is physically able to answer questions but refuses, I can get a court order. However, Judge Buckley is not due here for another week, and I would like to do it now. Perhaps I can be persuasive without being argumentative."

"Very well. If I have your word that you will do nothing to aggravate her condition, you can try."

The threat of a court order is what it took. Mrs. Mooreman was emphatic until the lawyer advised her that he could get an order from the judge and take a deposition from her with or without her permission. Finally, she agreed, providing that her friend could be present. A witness was exactly what Amos P. Sharp wanted.

"Now then," he said, standing while his secretary sat in the one wooden chair in the room, "will you please, Mrs. Mooreman, tell me what happened the day that Mr. Casey called upon the Reverend Weems?"

Her voice showed only a hint of weakness. "Well, we were in the rectory, the reverend and I, when Mr. Casey knocked on the door. The reverend never locked the door, and he said to come in. Mr. Casey was very angry. He accused the reverend of lying about him and accusing him of getting rich by cheating folks." Mrs. Mooreman paused as if trying to remember.

"Please go on."

"The reverend denied lying and said he believed Mr. Casey did intentionally profit from the misfortunes of others, and caused hardships on some folks by refusing water from the creeks. He said the rivers and streams were God's work and should be shared by all. He said Mr. Casey falsely accused honest hardworking family men of stealing his cattle, and he did it to try to force them off their land so he could buy their land cheap." Her lips tightened.

"And what did Mr. Casey say?"

"He called the reverend a liar, and accused him of misleading his congregation."

"Did he threaten the reverend?"

"I believe he did. I am convinced he did."

The lawyer kept his voice low, calm, and tried to talk as if he were talking to a friend. "Umm. Tell me, Mrs. Mooreman, what did Mr. Casey say?"

"Like I said in court, I can't recall his exact words. He was very angry, and he said . . . I recall him saying the town didn't need a man like the reverend." Mrs. Mooreman's voice picked up volume now as her mind took her back to that day. "He said the reverend should

150

be preaching the gospel instead of hatred, and the town would be better off without him."

The secretary was writing furiously while Mrs. Mooreman talked.

"The Reverend Weems said Mr. Casey was a disciple of the devil, and God would strike him down the way He struck down Mrs. Casey. He said the Indians were sent there by God, and . . ." The woman's voice was rising.

"Take your time, Mrs. Mooreman. Try to remember exactly what was said."

"Mr. Casey was so angry I thought he was going to strike the reverend. He yelled something. Then he left."

"What did he yell?"

"I . . . I was so fearful for the reverend, that I . . . didn't understand what he yelled."

"But you took it to be a threat on the reverend's life?"

"Yes. Mr. Casey was threatening."

"But—and this is important, Mrs. Mooreman—do you remember Mr. Casey actually saying anything threatening?"

"All I remember is Mr. Casey was very angry, and he took two or three steps toward the reverend with his fists doubled. I was so afraid for Reverend Weems, I . . ."

"What did the reverend do when Mr. Casey advanced on him?"

"The reverend was a brave man. He stood his ground."

"Then what happened?"

Mrs. Mooreman looked over at her friend and neighbor who was standing beside the bed. The woman took her hand, but said nothing. "Mr. Casey turned around and left. He slammed the door on his way out."

"Umm. Tell me, was Mr. Casey armed?"

"Yes, he was. He carried a pistol in a holster on his right side."

"A pistol. Umm. Mrs. Mooreman, I'm told that your late husband was in the freighting business. Did he carry a weapon?"

"He always carried a pistol. Most men carry a pistol."

"Then did Mr. Casey draw his pistol? Did he touch it in a threatening manner?"

"I don't believe he did."

"Umm." Amos P. Sharp looked at his secretary to see if she had it all down on paper. She nodded at him. "I have one more question, Mrs. Mooreman. You've told me more here today than you told the trial jury. Why?"

"I . . . because nobody asked as many questions then."

"Umm. I see. Well, I thank you kindly, Mrs. Mooreman. I do wish you a speedy recovery."

Outside, Dr. Woodrow had been joined by his assistant. She asked, "How did it go, Mr. Sharp?"

"It went well. I don't know whether the judge will consider this grounds for setting aside the verdict, but it will certainly help. On the other hand, he could admonish me for questioning a woman who is in her sick bed." The lawyer frowned at his feet. "I wish I could find something else. Anything." He looked at the doctor and at Ruth Ann. "This is my fault. I should have cross-examined her relentlessly when she was on the witness stand. But . . . I was afraid the jury would sympathize with her, and I thought her testimony was vague enough that the jury would lend it no credence. I was wrong."

No one said anything for a long moment. Then the lawyer added, "If nothing else works I will move for a new trial on the grounds that the defendant was . . ." He swallowed hard. "Was inadequately represented."

Ruth Ann touched his arm. "I'm sure you did the best you could."

Heads down, the lawyer and his secretary walked away toward their hotel. Dr. Woodrow went in to see his patient.

The short visit with the Reverend Weems was on Jim Casey's mind, too, as he rode back to the abandoned homestead. Why it came to mind now on top of everything else, he didn't know. But it did, vividly. He'd never in his life wanted to hit a man as badly as he'd wanted to hit the Reverend Weems. He'd never been angrier. If the reverend had been armed, Casey would have challenged him to a duel. How he'd managed to hold his anger down and leave the so-called rectory without beating that mealymouthed son of a bitch half to death, he didn't understand. Maybe because of that white collar, or because they were in a rectory, supposedly a House of God.

But how could that sorry piece of horse shit say Boots was a sinner and was struck down by God as punishment?

I didn't kill him, Casey thought, but I should have.

As he rode, Casey suddenly realized that every muscle in his body was tense, every nerve on edge. He had to forget it. The reverend was dead. Somebody else killed the sorry son of a bitch. Now the question was who? And the problem was to stay out of jail and save something of what he and Boots had worked for.

When he got back to the homestead, he found that Levi had been there and gone. A horse was hobbled near Indian Creek, a half mile from the homestead. Saddlebags full of groceries were hanging from the sagging

153

front door, and a penciled note was stuffed in with the groceries.

"Had to go to town and see the sheriff. Left a horse for yu. Be back tomorra A.M. Levi."

Casey ate, saddled the fresh horse, and rode up the Indian Creek Trail, leading the tired horse. There was only one thing to do. Keep trying. Gather more cattle. Out of four thousand head he ought to find three hundred. Make that four thousand less about two hundred.

Levi would know where to find him.

Sheriff Waltham Jackson was angry. Not at Levi, but because of what Levi had told him. "Cattle stealing is always a big problem for county sheriffs. The C Bar has already lost more than its share of cattle to rustlers." He leaned back in the chair at his desk. Statements from Levi and Mrs. Carter were on the desk, written and notarized by a clerk from the county government office.

Levi had lied a little. He'd told the sheriff he'd rounded up the cattle by himself. A cattleman would have known better, but Sheriff Jackson was no cattleman.

"Well, I'll do what I can," Jackson said. "I'll send a telegraph to the sheriff in Jefferson County and ask him to be on the lookout for cattle bearing the C Bar brand, and I'll get on their trail myself. They can't move a herd of cattle very far in a week or ten days, but they can get to the railroad pens in less time than that. Maybe I'll get lucky. I'll work on it."

It took a lot of hard riding from dawn to dark to gather a herd of cattle out of the canyons, rocky slopes, and narrow valleys west and north of the Indian Creek camp. Fortunately, Jim Casey and his hired man had enough horses to do it. They took turns carrying the long-barreled rifle, knowing there was no way to carry it horseback so it was comfortable without interfering with the movements of the horse.

Then came the long drive down out of the mountains. This time they stopped for a day in a narrow canyon where the cattle could only drift downhill. "We're gonna kill these horses if we don't let them rest and graze," Casey said.

"The only grass is along the crik, but there's enough."

Then, for the third time, they were out of the arroyos and off the talus slopes of the foothills. As before, they agreed that Levi would go to the ranch for supplies and to check on Mrs. Carter.

"I feel like a damned fool," Casey said. "We're doing the rustlers' work for them. We round up the cattle and push them down here on the flats, then leave them."

"Makes it easy for 'em," Levi allowed. "But I can't think of anything better to do."

"Maybe Sheriff Jackson—I'd bet anything he didn't catch any thieves—but maybe he went to Castle Rock and asked enough questions to put some fear into them."

"Might make 'em hold off for a while 'till things cool down."

"We can hope."

Levi had cached some tins of beans and fruit in the homestead shack, believing the airtight cans were the only chuck that mice and raccoons couldn't get into. For the first time, when Levi rode north, Casey had something to eat.

Mrs. Carter was happy to see the old man. She was lonely, and he was good company. Again he urged her to go to town and stay there. Again she refused. But she had news. Not good news, but something to talk about.

Sheriff Jackson had stopped at the ranch and told her about trailing the stolen cattle to Castle Rock, but getting there too late. The sheriff believed his ride was not in vain, however. He'd learned the name of the buyer, who'd come from Kansas for the purpose of buying cattle. The sellers had a bill of sale, forged, no doubt. No state brand inspector had been present. The bad news was that the cattle and the buyer were somewhere in Kansas now, and the cattle had no doubt been slaughtered. The sellers didn't stay around either.

Stuffing himself with hot biscuits, gravy, and canned ham, Levi said he didn't expect any good news. "I'll go to town and sniff around and see if anything's come up about the killin' of that preacher. There's always a chance there's somethin new."

"We surely could use some good news for a change," Mrs. Carter said.

This time the riders came from the north. Jim Casey saw them coming, and he saddled his horse and made himself visible. They stopped and talked among themselves, looking his way. Six of them. Then they came on. Casey checked the long-barreled, trap-door rifle. He'd put five rounds in his pocket, but he'd left the box of shells in a saddlebag which hung from a willow tree near the creek. He raised the trap door, shoved a round into the firing chamber, and dismounted.

One of the riders waved his hat at him and hollered something. The wave was supposed to be a friendly gesture, but Jim didn't trust them. He let them come closer, close enough that he could see their faces. Strangers. Holding the reins in his left hand, Casey fired a shot in the air, hoping to discourage them. The horse snorted and jerked back, but didn't jerk free. The riders stopped again, talked among themselves.

Suddenly, they drew six-guns, spurred their horses, and charged straight at Casey, firing as they came.

Chapter Twenty-One

He was too good a target, standing out in the open. He tried to lead the horse toward the shack, but the animal was pulling back, rearing, terrified at the sound of gunfire. Jim Casey had to drop the reins and run for cover. The riders were within six-gun range now, and the horse was sure to be hit unless Casey got away from it. He needed the horse.

Running for the shack, the only cover anywhere near, Casey heard the angry whine of lead bullets go past his head, saw them kick up dirt near his feet. Something hit him a hammer blow on his right side. It knocked him half around. He fell to his knees, picked himself up, and ran.

Inside the shack, he looked through the one window as bullets punched splintery holes in the thin wooden wall near him. He had to shoot back, but he was almost as good a target at the window as he was outside.

Casey dropped to the floor in the open doorway. Dropped flat, then raised up onto his elbows and sighted down the rifle barrel. Damned singleshot gun. He yanked open the trap door, threw an empty cartridge out, shoved another in, and slammed the loading door down.

Four of the men were on foot now, walking toward him, shooting. Bullets whined over his head. Bullets smashed into the broken floorboards. Casey aimed at a man, fired. The man dropped immediately. A lead slug plowed a furrow in the floor just under Casey's left elbow. He worked the loading trap again, aimed, fired. His target chose that instant to hit the ground, and the shot missed.

How many cartridges did he have left? Casey emptied his pocket. Two. He'd bought the damned gun to hunt meat with. It had more range and was more accurate than a short-barreled saddle rifle. But it sure wasn't made for a gunfight.

Two rifle shots left. The saddlebags at the creek held a box of cartridges, but it would be suicide to run out there. Casey had to make the two shots count.

The gunsels knew now that his rifle was more accurate than their six-guns, and they flattened themselves on the ground, firing from a prone position. Ignoring the lead whistling and slamming around him, Casey aimed at the top of a man's black hat, squeezed off another shot. The black hat rolled off the man's head. The man lay still.

Then bullets were coming from behind the shack. The shooters couldn't see Casey through the thin back wall, but they knew where he was and they fired shots through the boards, hoping one would find him.

Goddam. Casey rolled onto his back, drew the Navy Colt, and fired two shots through the wall. He looked out the door again in time to see a gunman raise up on one knee, hold his right wrist with his left hand, squint down the barrel of his six-gun. Casey rolled at the instant a bullet kicked up splinters in the floor right where he'd been.

Son of a bitch. He dropped the Colt, loaded and

aimed the rifle and fired. It was a hasty shot, and Casey cursed himself for wasting his last rifle cartridge. But the gunman suddenly dropped his pistol, grabbed his right arm, and kneeled with his head touching the ground, obviously in pain.

The shooting stopped.

Nothing happened. Nothing moved. The quiet was as disturbing as the sound of gunfire.

Then men out there were running away, running for their horses. The one holding his arm, got up and ran in staggering steps for a horse. Casey could have shot him in the back with the Colt, but he didn't. He held the six-gun ready, but soon realized he was alone.

Except for two men. Two men out there were dead or dying.

Not until then did Casey feel the pain in his right side. On his knees now, he looked down at himself and saw blood covering the side of his shirt. With fumbling fingers, afraid of what he might see, he unbuttoned his shirt. The bullet had hit him about six inches above the belt, making a round hole. Blood was running out of the hole.

He had to put something over it and try to stop the bleeding. His shirt was all he had. Tearing it off, he wadded it and pressed it to the wound. He pulled his leather belt from his pants and used it to hold the wadded shirt in place. Then he stood and went looking for a horse.

The gunmen had taken all their horses, but Casey's horse was standing a hundred yards from the cabin. While he walked over there, Casey realized that the bullet had hit him in the back and had gone through him. That meant there was another bullet hole in his back. Reaching around with his left hand, he found it. His fingers came away bloody, but that hole wasn't bleeding as badly as the wound in front.

Bullets, he knew, sometimes did more damage coming out than going in. He was hurt. He needed help.

The horse snorted, took a few steps, then stopped and watched him come. "Whoa, feller. Rounder is your name, ain't it. Whoa Rounder."

Bare chested, trying to hold his right elbow against the wadded shirt, Casey climbed awkwardly into the saddle. The horse was one that Levi had brought from headquarters. He would know the way back.

"All right, Rounder." Casey started the horse in the right direction. "I apologize for working you so hard, Rounder. I need your help. Take me home."

Levi was feeling glum. He'd just come from the sheriff's office and was none the wiser for having been there. Sheriff Jackson had no news. The lawyer, Amos P. Sharp, had been in town, but had left again without saying anything to the sheriff. What to do? Maybe the boss ought to hire a Pinkerton detective. If Levi knew how to go about it he'd hire a detective himself, pay him out of his own pocket. How did a man go about hiring a detective? Hell, he'd spent a good part of his life trying to stay away from them, not hire them. Silently, he swore, hell's fire, goddamit.

"Good morning, Mr. Levi."

His head had been so full of worries that he didn't notice anyone else on the plank walk. Looking up, he recognized the pretty young woman who worked for Dr. Woodrow. Her blond hair had been brushed until it shone like sunlight. Her long yellow dress was fresh and crisp. He touched his hat brim.

"Mornin', Miss Abraham."

Her sunny smile turned to a frown. "You look terribly unhappy."

"Well, uh . . ." He didn't know what to say.

"Is there anything I can do? I owe you, you know."

"There's nothing, miss. Call me Levi. Nobody calls me mister."

"Sure, Levi." She smiled again, trying to cheer him up. "Would you like a cup of coffee? We can go to the doctor's house and I'll put the coffeepot on."

"Well, I . . ."

"Come on, Levi. I might even put a few drops of whiskey in it. The doctor never touches it, but he keeps a bottle in his cupboard for some reason or other."

"Well . . ."

"Oh, come on, Levi." Smiling, she looped her arm through his and led the way.

It was a strange experience for him, walking side by side, arm in arm, with a pretty young woman. He'd never done that before, and he felt badly out of place. But it was a good experience, too. It gave his spirits a boost. At the clinic, he followed her inside, removing his hat as he went through the door. His nearly bald head was unbelievably white in contrast to the dark, old leather color of his face.

"The doctor is visiting a home-bound patient," Ruth Ann said. "Come in the kitchen and sit at the table. It will take only a moment to brew some fresh coffee."

He sat and watched her work, putting a stick of split pine in the stove, measuring coffee grounds, pouring it and some water into a galvanized pot. Just watching her was a pleasure.

While they waited for the coffee to perk, she sat across the table from him. "Judging from what I've heard, you're being very loyal to your employer. That's most admirable."

162

"He's been good to me. Him and his late wife."

"He's innocent, isn't he? And that's why you're feeling so low."

"Plumb innocent."

Worry clouded her pale blue eyes, and she shook her head sadly. "I wish I could help. The doctor also believes Mr. Casey is innocent."

"The doctor done what he had to do in the trial. Said what he had to say." Levi was silent a moment, then, "Come to think of it he acted like he wanted to say somethin' else, but they cut 'im off."

"Oh." Ruth Ann suddenly sat up straighter. "I know what it was. Excuse me a moment, will you." She stood and left the room. When she returned she was carrying a shirt. "This, Levi, is the shirt the Reverend Weems was wearing when he was shot. Dr. Woodrow saved it." She spread it wide for his inspection.

Levi swallowed with a bobbing of his Adam's apple. "Yeah, I can see the bullet hole. Not much blood."

"The reverend was killed almost instantly, I believe. When the heart stops pumping, the bleeding stops. Do you notice anything else about this shirt?"

"It was burned a little around the bullet hole."

"Could that be important? Dr. Woodrow thought it could be, but he didn't know for sure, and I don't know either."

Then the old man's eyes brightened. His leathery, wrinkled face lit up. "Yeah, I mean yes, ma'am—miss. I b'lieve it is important."

"What's important about it, Levi?"

"It means the shooter had a black powder, cap and ball pistol. You put a few grains too much powder in an old cannon like mine and it'll shoot some fire."

"Is that the kind of gun Mr. Casey uses?"

"No. He carries a Navy Colt, .36 caliber, fixed to shoot the self-contained metal cartridges." Levi felt excitement rise in his chest. The coffee was percolating, but he didn't notice. "His gun wouldn't set that shirt on fire. In the dark, you might see a muzzle flash, but it wouldn't shoot enough fire to burn anything."

"Then, either Mr. Casey didn't shoot the Reverend Weems, or he used a gun different from the one he usually carries."

"No. No, ma'am. That Navy Colt is the onliest pistola I ever knowed him to carry." Levi took his own heavy gun from its holster and laid it carefully on the table. "Just so you'll know what it looks like, this is a black powder six-shooter. It takes a while to load it."

She didn't touch the gun, only looked at it. Levi put it away.

Folding the shirt, Ruth Ann again sat across from the old man. "Tell me, Levi, where is the gun that Mr. Casey was carrying when he was arrested?"

"The sheriff's got it."

"Then we have some evidence that wasn't presented in court." She crossed her arms, leaned forward, and looked into the old man's face. "This is very important, isn't it? We have to ... the lawyer, Mr. Sharp was in town, but he's gone back to Denver now. We have to tell him about this. I'll telegraph him. Yes." Ruth Ann straightened in her chair. "I'll do it right now. I'll send him a telegraph and tell him we have some new evidence."

Levi stood. "Me, I'm gonna hunt up Jim and give 'im some good news for a change. Whups. I didn't say that, did I? I'm not s'posed to know where he's at."

"I won't tell."

Walking fast, excitement within him, Levi went to his horse, mounted. He'd stop at headquarters and pick up some chuck, then catch a fresh horse and get back to Jim at a high lope.

Chapter Twenty-Two

It was dusk. Or was Jim Casey losing consciousness? He'd wrapped the reins around the saddle horn, let them hang slack, and depended on the horse to keep going in the right direction. Hanging on to the saddle horn with both hands, Casey knew he would soon become too weak to stay in the saddle. Mumbling, he talked to his late wife.

"It ain't easy, Boots, but we never had it easy, did we. We took whatever was thrown at us and just went on. I'm going on, Boots. It ain't easy, but I'm going on."

With each beat of his heart his wound throbbed. Well hell, he thought wryly, at least my heart is still beating. Holding his right elbow against the wadded shirt, he rode on.

Was that a rider over there? Or was he seeing things? In the gloom of late evening, it looked like a rider or a horse or a cow. Just wishful thinking. Keep moving, Rounder.

Then Levi was beside him. "Jim, what happened? Are you hurt?"

Through tight jaws, Casey mumbled, "Yeah, Levi, I'm hurt. I've been shot."

Ruth Ann had missed supper at the boardinghouse. Dr. Woodrow had had no supper either. They'd planned to close the door to the clinic shortly after sundown, but things happened.

First it was a man who came in leaning heavily on his wife and hopping on one foot. He'd accidentally shot himself in the other foot, he explained. It took an hour to dig out the lead and fragments of bone. Ruth Ann did the bandaging. She gave some cotton bandage material, some carbolic soap, and instructions to the wife. "Change the bandage every day and wash the wound thoroughly."

After that patient left, Dr. Woodrow suggested they go to the cafe for supper. They didn't get there. A four-year-old girl was carried in by her father. She'd suffered a compound fracture of the ulna in the left forearm. An injection of morphia numbed the arm while the doctor carefully set the bone in place. The child sniffed repeatedly, but cried very little. With Ruth Ann's help, Dr. Woodrow wrapped the arm tight enough to hold the bone in place, but not so tight as to hamper blood circulation. Then Ruth Ann mixed some plaster and the two of them covered the arm with a thick layer. After fashioning a sling, Ruth Ann ended the treatment by giving the child a kiss on the forehead.

"This is something you can tell your friends about," she said.

By now, it was past the cafe's closing time. Ruth Ann said she would find something to cook in the doctor's kitchen. She didn't even get that far.

They both knew from experience, when they heard the horse's hooves pounding down the street toward them, that it meant more work. Sure enough, the hooves jabbed the ground in a sudden stop in front of the clinic. Boots pounding the boardwalk.

"Here we go again," Ruth Ann said.

Levi burst through the door. "It's Jim Casey. He's been shot. He needs you, Doctor. Fast. I'll go hitch up your horse." Then he was out the door, horseback again, and riding at a dead run for the freight pens.

While he was gone, Dr. Woodrow packed his satchel, checking off each item. Scalpel. Probe. Forceps. Syringe. Small bottle of morphine. Carbolic soap. Spool of very fine silk thread. A short length of cat gut. Curved needles. Chloroform and inhaler.

"You don't have to go, Ruth Ann."

"I'll go."

Levi was back. "I left my horse at the pens. I hitched up a team instead of your buggy horse. We gotta hurry." Then they were in the buggy with one spring seat and a canopy, Ruth Ann jammed between the two men. Levi handled the lines. He clucked, then yelled at the two horses, and they left town on a gallop, the buggy swaying like a fish's tail.

It wasn't the first time Dr. Woodrow had made a hurried trip to the C Bar ranch. Three years ago, approximately, he'd been on the same emergency trip with Levi handling the lines. Then they were in a one-horse buggy, and it was Mrs. Casey who'd been shot.

He'd known, when he saw how deeply embedded the arrow was, that she was dying. The spleen had been ruptured. She was bleeding inside. In fact, he didn't understand why she was alive when he reached her.

The forceps he'd used then were invented by an Army surgeon who'd extracted arrows before. Dr. Woodrow had given Mrs. Casey a large dose of morphia to stop the pain, then inserted the forceps. Arrow blades were often extremely difficult to extract. Because of the way they were shaped, they often did more damage to the tissues and organs when they were taken out. They were difficult to grasp with most forceps.

Dr. Woodrow had used a scissorslike instrument, and he'd forced it deep enough into the wound to clamp it onto the bottom of the blade.

But Mrs. Casey died soon after. The morphia had let her die in her sleep.

The young doctor had served his time in the hospital's dead house. He'd cut into his share of cadavers. He'd served his time in the hospital's emergency room. Breaking the sad news to grieving families would be part of his life until he retired. A doctor had to be immune to it.

But the grief in that ranch house was almost more than he could bear. The husband was so emotional he couldn't talk. Old Levi, as rugged a man as the doctor had ever met, had to continually wipe his eyes and blow his nose on a bandana. Mrs. Carter had wept openly.

Driving back to town that night, the horse moving at a walk, young Dr. Woodrow felt as though a black shroud of gloom was wrapped around him. The world was a dark, gloomy place. He wished he could have saved her. Lord, he wished he could have saved her.

Three days later, Mr. Casey came to town to pay him. And brought him a beautiful sorrel gelding, sleek and gentle. "He's yours, Doctor. When you have to go somewhere horseback, ride him. He's got a lope that's so smooth and easy you can carry a cup of coffee on him."

Now the doctor was making another emergency run to the C Bar ranch. Under his breath he pleaded: Don't let it end that way this time. Lord, don't let it end that way.

The patient was lying on his side in a downstairs bedroom, nude except for his shorts, covered to the waist with a clean white sheet. He was conscious, but his face was pale and his voice was weak. He'd lost blood. The bullet had entered his back between the hip bone and the lower rib. It had gone completely through, missing the vertebra by a wide margin, but probably lacerating the ascending colon. The colon could be repaired.

"We need more light," Dr. Woodrow said, "and some boiling water."

Levi said, "I'll get a bull's-eye lantern," and he hurried out.

"I'll boil some water and bring more lamps," Mrs. Carter said.

Ruth Ann asked, "How does it look, Doctor?"

"It missed the vital organs. There's no lead or bone fragments to probe for. I'll have to make an incision to inspect the colon for damage, and I'll have to tie off some blood vessels. He'll be weak, but if no complications arise, he should recover."

Because chloroform was highly inflammable and because of so many lamps, Dr. Woodrow decided to give the patient an injection of morphine. That wouldn't put him to sleep, but it would lessen the pain.

While Levi held the bull's-eye lantern, the doctor examined the wound more closely. Then he took his scalpel from a pot of hot water and carefully opened the patient's side. Using a speculum to hold the incision open, he sutured the lacerated section of the colon with the cat gut. "This will decompose," he said to everyone present. That done, he tied two blood vessels with the remainder of the cat gut, then straightened up.

"You can wash the wound now," he said to Ruth Ann. She worked up a lather with the carbolic soap and thoroughly washed the wound inside and out. The doctor removed the speculum.

Casey's eyes blinked, but otherwise he showed no sign of consciousness.

When Ruth Ann finished, the doctor took six stitches to close the incision. He asked, "Are you awake, Mr. Casey?"

"Unnh," Casey said.

"Barring complications, such as infection, you'll be fine. I'm not going to close the wound entirely. I prefer to let it drain."

Voice weak, Casey tried to joke: "I must be living right."

"You're a strong man. You seem to be a little undernourished, but otherwise in good health. Keep the wound clean, change the dressings twice a day, and you will be on your feet in, oh, a month or two."

Mrs. Carter spoke, "He won't be undernourished anymore. Not as long as he stays here. I can fix him any kind of food you recommend, Doctor."

Ruth Ann bandaged the wounds, and handed Mrs. Carter a roll of soft cotton, a bar of carbolic soap, and a bottle of yellowish laudanum for pain. Talk of food reminded her that she hadn't eaten since noon, but she said nothing about that.

"I'm going to give you a drink of bromide now, Mr. Casey. It will help you sleep. You need a lot of sleep and rest."

They watched Casey drink the bromide, turn onto his left side, and close his eyes. Ruth Ann covered him to

171

his ears with the white sheet. As they left the room, carrying lamps, Mrs. Carter said, "You both must be awfully tired. Would you care for an early breakfast?"

Boy, Ruth Ann thought, would I ever.

Chapter Twenty-Three

Rain finally came to the eastern slopes of Colorado, and Levi wore his long yellow slicker when he rode south. He appreciated the rain, and didn't mind rain water running down the neck of the slicker, soaking his shoulders and back. The weather had been too dry. The rain was just what the grass needed before the high country's short growing season ended. Levi led two horses and carried two saddlebags of groceries, planning to spend some time on the south end of the C Bar holdings.

When he got to the abandoned homestead, two saddled horses were standing there, hobbled. Two men wearing slickers like his watched him come.

"Mornin', Sheriff, Deputy Rankin. See you're gettin' around early."

"We wanted to locate the bodies before the coyotes and magpies did," Sheriff Waltham Jackson said.

Dismounting, Levi said, "Glad you found my rifle. I was in such a hurry to get away from here, I left it behind."

Sheriff Jackson stepped in front of him, faced him, hands on hips. "You left it behind, did you?"

"Yup." The old man's Adam's apple bobbed.

Deputy Rankin said nothing, just watched and listened.

"Strange." The sheriff's eyes were fixed on Levi's face. "There's blood on the floor of the shack over there. I don't see any wounds on you. Who bled?"

"Why, uh, the one I shot in the arm."

"He go in there after you shot him, did he?"

"I guess he thought I was still in there. I snuck out when they wasn't watchin'."

Looking away now, Sheriff Jackson let his eyes rove over the country, the scraggly line of willow trees along Indian Creek, the cattle, the mountains to the west with clouds moving over them. Then he said, "I believe it's going to clear up." He was silent a moment, then, "Well, the cattle you said you rounded up all by yourself are still here. The would-be rustlers, whoever they are, got nothing but a dose of death for their trouble."

"I'm sure tickled the cattle ain't quit the country."

"Hmm. That makes, let's see, two you shot and killed at the ranch house and two here. Four."

"It ain't somethin' I'd brag about."

"Hmm." Jackson turned and walked away, head down. He walked in a big circle and came back. He stopped in front of Levi, hands on hips again. "How is Jim Casey? Is he hurt bad?"

"Huh?" Levi's Adam's apple went up and down his throat.

"It was Jim Casey who shot these two, and he was shot himself. Is he hurt bad?"

When Levi didn't answer immediately, the sheriff looked down at his boots. He believed he had legal cause to arrest the old man for lying about a possible crime. But he wouldn't. The old gent was being loyal to his boss, and he wouldn't arrest a man for that. "You know, Levi, I suspected you were lying to me when you reported this shooting. I've been told about the doctor leaving town in a hell of a hurry with you driving the team. I haven't gone to the ranch house yet, but I will. Tell me—honest now—was Jim Casey hurt very bad?"

No use lying anymore. Levi looked the sheriff in the eye. "He was hit in the side. The doctor said he'll get well if nothin' else happens."

"Uh-huh. Hmm."

"You gonna arrest 'im?"

"When he's able to move. I'm not gonna arrest you. You've got work to do."

"I 'preciate that."

"Go on about your work, Levi." The sheriff shook his head sadly. "You've sure got a lot of it."

Now that the rain was over, the day was beautiful. Dr. Woodrow was enjoying himself, riding the easy-gaited sorrel gelding, carrying his leather medicine boxes made to fit across the saddle fork. It was good to get out of town on a sunny day. The air smelled clean and fresh, and the horse seemed to be enjoying the trip, too. Of course, the clinic was always on his mind, but now that he had an assistant he wasn't afraid to be gone for a few hours. Ruth Ann could set a fractured bone if necessary, and she knew how to inject morphine to deaden the pain. Writing prescriptions was something she could not do, nor could she perform surgery. But she could administer patent medicine or the "granny medicine," as she called it.

While most doctors were disdainful of granny medicine, Dr. Woodrow had seen some that actually helped patients. He had seen wood ashes and cobwebs stop bleeding, and a mashed potato poultice used to draw out the core of a boil. When professional attention wasn't available granny medicine was often better than nothing.

Why, it wasn't long ago that an Army doctor had saved an Indian woman's life with mouth-to-mouth resuscitation.

As Dr. Woodrow rode at a comfortable slow trot into the ranch yard, he noted how quiet it was. Mrs. Carter was looking out a kitchen window at him, and when she recognized him, she opened the door and stepped outside to greet him.

"Good morning, Mrs. Carter. Fine day, isn't it?"

"Good mornin', Doctor. Tie up your horse and come in. Mr. Casey is feeling better this morning. I think the rain made him feel better."

With his saddle boxes in his hand, the doctor entered the kitchen where he smelled something delicious. "How is his appetite, Mrs. Carter?"

"He's eating good. I've fed him all kinds of soup— potato soup, bean soup, bacon soup, sausage soup. He cleans the bowl."

"He's very fortunate to have such a good cook."

Casey heard the conversation. Quickly, he straightened the bed covers and raised up enough to fluff the pillow. When the doctor came into the room, he grinned. "Thought I heard your friendly voice out in the kitchen. Stay for dinner. Mrs. Carter's got some sausage soup that'll make a sick man get out of bed and catch rabbits on foot."

"You've got some color back in your face. How do you feel?"

"Finer than the fur on a cat's back."

"Unn-huh. Here, take this under your tongue." While the thermometer was registering the patient's temperature, Dr. Woodrow checked his pulse. Smiling, he said,

"Don't talk now, not until I remove the thermometer, but then I want you to give me an honest answer. It's important. Understand?"

Casey nodded.

After removing the thermometer, the doctor held it up to the window light, said, "Um-huh," then, "All right now, how do you feel?"

"Well, I don't much feel like chasing rabbits, but . . ."

"Your stomach. Do you feel any pain in your stomach?"

"Well . . ."

"Does it hurt while you are eating or after?"

"After."

"Unn-huh. I expect the colon is still sore and it hurts when you are digesting. That's to be expected. Now let's have a look."

A few minutes later, he straightened. "I see no complications. How are your bowel movements?"

"Unnh."

"You are emptying your bowels?"

Casey nodded.

"And you are not walking to the toilet?"

Casey shook his head.

Noticing Mrs. Carter standing in the open doorway, the doctor gave her a questioning look.

"I do what needs to be done," she said. "He don't like it but he wants to get well."

"You are very fortunate, Mr. Casey, to have such a fine nurse."

The patient was right. Mrs. Carter's sausage soup was delicious. Dr. Woodrow was pleased with everything when he rode back to town. The patient was doing as well as could be expected, he had a good meal under his belt, and the ride was pleasant. "You're a good horse,

Redwing," he said, reaching down and patting the animal's neck.

It was not until he rode down First Street that he had something to worry about.

Sheriff Waltham Jackson stepped into the street in front of him, and said, "I need to talk to you about something, Doctor. Can you spare me a minute?"

Dr. Woodrow, dismounted, tied up, and followed the sheriff into his office. "Sit down, Doctor." The sheriff nodded at one of the two chairs in his office. "Let me ask you, how is Jim Casey doing?"

For a moment, Dr. Woodrow didn't know how to answer. He was surprised that the sheriff knew about Mr. Casey's wound. But now that he obviously did know, the only thing he could say was the truth.

"I believe he will recover. He is still weak, and he cannot, should not, be moved."

"When do you think we can move him?"

"That's hard to say. Not for a week, at least. Are you going to incarcerate him?"

"Of course. I have to. But not until you say it's safe to move him."

"It is definitely not safe yet."

Sheriff Jackson leaned back in his chair and folded his hands across his belly. "I'll make a deal with you Doctor. I'll . . . you know what worries me? Jim Casey knows by now that I know where he is. His hired man, Levi, has no doubt told him by now. I'm scared he'll jump up and run before he's well enough."

"Oh no." Dr. Woodrow shook his head. "That would be dangerous. It could be fatal."

"I'll make a deal with you, then. I won't bother him. I won't even go out there if you promise to tell me when he can be moved as soon as he can be moved."

Spreading his hands, shaking his head sadly, the doctor said, "If that is the way it must be . . . yes, I will keep you informed. Then Mr. Casey is definitely going back to jail?"

"Yessir. Jim Casey has to be locked up."

Chapter Twenty-Four

Jim Casey had reached a decision: he was through running. The only way he could stop running and clear his name was to give himself up. Levi had told him about the burns around the bullet hole in the shirt the Reverend Weems was wearing, and about the statement Amos Sharp had taken from Agnes Mooreman. Surely, he would get a new trial, and surely the trial would be moved to Denver or Colorado Springs where an impartial jury could be found.

Meanwhile, with any luck at all, he would be held in the Rockledge jail instead of taken to the penitentiary, and from there he could write checks on his account in the Farmers State Bank. Levi could hire a few men to help gather enough cattle to pay off the bank note. He could even delegate enough authority to Levi that he could sell the cattle.

With any luck at all.

Dammit, that judge just had to listen to reason and grant him a new trial. If he didn't, and sentenced him to hang or to prison, it was all hopeless.

Dr. Woodrow came twice more, and the second time solemnly advised Casey about his agreement with the sheriff. "Don't worry about it," Casey said. "I was planning to give myself up anyway."

"I can visit you in jail," the doctor said, "and see that you heal properly."

Forcing a grin, Casey said, "There's always something to be thankful for."

There was no excitement on the streets, no on-lookers when Jim Casey climbed sorely down from the buggy and walked, bent slightly at the waist, into the sheriff's office. Sheriff Jackson had been told he was coming, and hadn't told anyone else. And Levi had already brought some blankets and a pillow. The sheriff had agreed to allow Mrs. Carter to bring him some soup, the kind of food that was easy to digest.

Casey made himself comfortable on the jail bunk, glad to lie down again. He frowned when the cell was locked, reminding him that he was a prisoner in a cage. But in his mind he tried to be optimistic. The stitches had been cut from his side yesterday, and he would heal faster now. Amos Sharp had promised to be in town tomorrow and would file his motion for a new trial. Levi had managed to gather about seventy-five more cattle from the foothills west of Squaw Mountain, and would soon be traveling by train to Denver to look for a buyer and to hire two cowboys. And, now that four men had been killed trying to steal from the C Bar, the thieves might stay away.

It was Levi who was the pessimist. "I ain't had no traffic with honest cow buyers," he'd said. "I don't know nothin' about the business end of runnin' a ranch. I don't know what cattle are worth. I ain't never hired a man in my life."

"You're not dumb, Levi," Casey had said. "You can ask at the Union stockyards and get an idea what the cattle market is. You've traded horses. You sell cattle the same way. You dicker. As for hiring men, you know as much about men as I do. Maybe more. The lawyer, Amos Sharp, will draw up a paper for me to sign giving you all the authority you need."

"I'll take a shot at it, Jim, but . . ."

"Tell you what, Levi. I'll send enough money with you that you can stay in the best hotel in Denver and eat at one of the best restaurants. Have yourself a shindig."

"Shore, Jim."

Amos P. Sharp was right on time, looking the successful lawyer in his boiled white shirt, cravat at his throat, and Prince Albert coat. "Judge Buckley will be in town tomorrow," he said. "There's very little on his docket. Sheriff Jackson has had a look at the shirt the Reverend Weems was wearing when he was shot, and he agreed with your man Levi that the shot was fired from a, uh, black powder weapon, and he said he'd testify that the gun he took from you could not have fired the shot. I have a statement from Mrs. Mooreman. It looks good."

"Fine. Good work, Amos. Now I need you to draw up whatever kind of paper it takes to give Levi authority to sell cattle for me."

Then Mrs. Carter came to town in the one-horse buggy, and brought him a lard can full of beef soup and some fresh-baked bread. The gallon lard can had been scoured clean before it was filled with soup, and wrapped in a piece of blanket to keep it warm. After dinner Levi came in to pick up the letter of authority. He said he'd ride to Jack's Corners in the morning and get on the train to Denver. Dr. Woodrow came in and looked at Casey's wound, seemed satisfied, and left. Todd Shipley, president of the Farmers State Bank, came in, too. He showed Casey that he had enough money in his account to hire a few men and buy a few horses. Tudor Howell of Howell Mercantile came over to inform him that Mrs. Carter or Levi could take whatever groceries they needed on credit. "If it hadn't been for the C Bar my business prob'ly wouldn't have lasted," he said.

Casey grinned, "Tell that to the rest of the county, will you?"

"I been tellin' them. Some of the men might believe me but the women won't. They thought the sun rose and set on that preacher."

Even Sheriff Jackson was all smiles. "That grub sure smells good. Your cook is saving the county some money."

Casey had a question: "Did that prosecutor show up?"

"Yep. He's here. He said he's gonna argue against a new trial."

Frowning, Casey said, "Sure, sure."

"I don't know much about the law. We've never had a murder case here before. But I ain't got nothing bad to say about you."

"I appreciate that."

Casey slept well that night.

But in the morning he began worrying. His breakfast from the cafe sat heavy on his stomach, his side was aching, and he couldn't help looking on the sour side of everything. What would happen if the judge denied him a new trial? How could a man's life, everything he owned, be pinned on one man's decision? Would he be hung? No, surely he wouldn't be hung while an appeal to the higher courts was pending. Would he? But he could be taken to the penitentiary right away. The county honchos didn't like to keep prisoners in the county jail. That cost too much.

Thinking about it made Casey nervous. He wished he could be there when his case was argued. All he could do was sit here and leave it up to a lawyer. Amos Sharp was doing his best, Casey believed, but having to leave everything up to someone else was worrisome. The hearing was scheduled for ten o'clock. He had a long time to wait and worry.

Jim Casey sat on the bunk with his head in his hands, staring at the floor. "This isn't like the other problems we had, Boots," he mumbled. "Then we could do something instead of just sit and depend on other folks. It's gonna be all right, isn't it, Boots? Lord, I wish you could talk to me and tell me it's gonna be all right."

Mrs. Carter was back in town at noon with fresh bread, apple butter, and bacon soup. She was cheerful. "At least we know you're not running around and tearing up your side. And Mr. Howell over at the mercantile told me to make up a list of everything I need, and he'll bill you for it later. He seems to think you're gonna be out of here pretty soon."

Her cheerfulness didn't rub off on Casey. "Yeah, that ain't what he told me. He said if the women in this sodbuster county had their way I'd be in my grave."

"Well." Mrs. Carter's smile was replaced by a frown. "To tell the truth about it, some of the ladies I met at the store acted like I was dirt under their feet."

"That preacher sure had the women halterbroke. And most of the men."

"I don't let 'em bother me. I know you didn't do anything bad, and I just pretend I don't hear 'em."

"Did Levi get started this morning?"

"Yes. He left horseback. He had that letter the lawyer

wrote and some U.S. greenbacks. He said he's gonna leave his horse at Jack's Corners."

"I wish you'd stay in town, Mrs. Carter. It's not safe at the ranch house for a woman alone."

"Me and Levi talked about that again last night. We believe it's safer now than it was before he shot them two stealers. And I've got that Winchester rifle, and I know how to use it."

"I sure do appreciate everything, Mrs. Carter. I hope to be able to make it up to you and Levi."

"Don't you worry about that. Don't even think about it. You've got other things to think about now."

After she left, he silently agreed with her. He had other things to worry about. He wished he'd asked her what time it was. Dammit, a man couldn't even see the sun from a jail. Hell, it could be the middle of the afternoon. It had to be at least noon.

He ought to hear something any minute now.

Chapter Twenty-Five

Instead of news from the courtroom, he got a cell-mate. A drunk. Deputy Rankin half-dragged him in and shoved him through the cell door. The deputy didn't draw his six-gun this time. He had his hands full with the drunk, and he knew Casey was in no condition to run anyway.

"If he bothers you, holler," Rankin said to Casey.

Casey grumbled, "Just what I need."

His cellmate was middle-aged with a full brown beard, squinty eyes, and thinning hair. He wore slouchy faded bib overalls and badly worn brogan shoes that should have been thrown away. "Shit. Goddamnit." He tried to shake the jail bars with both hands, but the bars wouldn't yield. He yelled, "What the goddam hell's wrong with this goddam town anyhow? Cain't a man take a drink of likker 'thout gettin' his ass throwed in jail?"

Turning his attention to Casey, he said, "What the hell you starin' at? And how come you got blankets and a pillow and there ain't none on the other bunk?"

Casey said nothing, but he pulled his boots on in case he had to defend himself.

"Goddam laws. Just wait for a man to come to town

with some spendin' money so's they can lock 'im up and take it away from 'im. What the goddam hell you in here for?"

"Murder."

That got the drunk's attention. "What? Murder? Well, I'll be goddamned." He burped, and Casey could smell the whiskey on his breath clear across the cell. "Who'd you kill?"

"Nobody."

"Nobody? You didn't kill nobody but you're in jail for killin' somebody?"

"Correct."

"Shit, ever'body that kills somebody says he didn't kill nobody."

Casey said nothing.

"What's your"—*burp*—"name?"

"What's yours?"

"Name's Howdy. And"—*burp*—"don't make no smartass jokes about it neither 'cuz thas my name and nobody that don't like it better put up his dukes."

"I've heard stranger names."

"Well, what's your name?"

"Casey."

"Casey?" The drunk's bearded face screwed up in concentration. "I heerd that name afore." Then a puzzled look came over the face. "Casey. You ain't . . . you . . . you ain't Jim Casey, the feller that killed that there preacher?"

"I'm Jim Casey."

"Well, I'll be a sumbitch." The expression changed from puzzled to angry. "My boss knows you. He said that preacher feller was right. He said you hogged all the water in these parts and you're tryin' to kick the farmers off their land so's you can buy it cheap."

187

Shrugging, Casey said, "This is just not good farm country."

"Hell it ain't. It would be if we could take some water out'n the crik."

"Are you a farmer?"

"I work for a farmer. 'Least I did. He fired me when his corn didn't grow."

"It's been too dry to grow anything but wild grass. I used to try to tell the settlers that."

"Shore you did. You're just what my boss said. You're tryin' to chase ever'body off so's you can have it all."

Suddenly, Casey felt like a fool. Why was he trying to explain it to this drunk who wouldn't believe anything he said anyway? He lay back on his bunk and closed his eyes.

"I oughtta kick the shit out'n you just for gen'ral principles. You rich sumbitches think you oughtta own the goddam world."

Casey opened his eyes then and watched the drunk. He knew he was in no condition to fight. Not with his fists. What he would do, he decided, was kick. If the drunk charged him he'd aim for the crotch with one boot and the face with the other. Maybe the man was drunk enough that he'd leave himself wide open for a couple of solid kicks.

But the bearded drunk sat on the other bunk and put his head in his hands. "Goddam laws. Goddam town. Goddam ever'body." His voice was becoming more and more slurred, and his eyes were getting heavy. "Shit fire and save matches. Goddam ever'thing."

Slowly, he sank back on his bunk. His mouth opened, showing brown, broken teeth. He started snoring.

Casey relaxed. Tried to. Any minute now he'd know more about his future. Thinking of that again got his

188

heart pumping too fast. He tried to get his mind off it. Think of something else. That drunk, what he'd said. There was some truth in it. Sure, he'd tried to discourage two homesteaders. He and Boots had always known that whoever controlled the water controlled the land, and they'd bought land along the creeks. They knew too that in spite of all the summer showers and lightning storms and snow in the winter that this was a semiarid climate. Someone once said all land west of the twenty-inch rainfall line that ran north and south through western Kansas wasn't suitable for farming. Casey knew it was true. Still, they came.

He remembered one family that had stopped by the ranch house to fill their water barrel and water their team. A man, his wife, and three towheaded kids. Everything they owned was piled on a wagon pulled by a tired horse and a mule. He'd tried to give them some sound advice. "Go up to Denver and get a job so you can take care of your family. You'll starve trying to farm in this country."

Instead of thanks, he got a cursing. "You land grabbers are all alike. You just want ever'body else to stay away so you can have it all." Even the woman had put in her opinion. "There's a hot place in the hereafter for people like you." One of the kids stuck out his tongue at him.

The second family he'd tried to advise was equally as grateful. He and Boots kept their advice to themselves after that. And while they allowed the sodbusters to carry water from the creeks by the barrelfuls, they wouldn't talk about irrigation. Irrigation wouldn't grow crops in this climate and soil anyway.

The connecting door opened. Amos P. Sharp came through. Casey stood, breathing in shallow breaths, his heart pounding. The lawyer's face told him nothing.

"We won and we lost."

"What happened?"

"We get a new trial, but we don't get a change of venue."

"Well ... well, don't you think I'll be acquitted now, what with new evidence and all?"

"I don't know. Your chances have improved. But the general feeling in this county—as best as I can determine—is you're guilty. I had a conversation with Sheriff Jackson, and it's his opinion that most folks think Mrs. Mooreman is too sick to think straight now, and I took an unfair advantage of her."

"I guess everybody knows about Mrs. Mooreman's statement to you."

"Word got around. I don't know how. Well, I can guess. One of her neighbors was present at the time."

"What about the burned shirt?"

"The prosecutor said you could have used another gun, possibly the gun your employee carries. That's what he'll say in the new trial."

"Aw for ..." Casey's heart dropped into his stomach. All he could do was shake his head.

"I really argued hard for a change of venue. I really think the judge should have granted that."

Bitterness was welling up in Casey now. "Everything depends on what one man rules. One appointed son of a bitch."

"I'm afraid so."

"Aw shit. Excuse my language, but another trial is a waste of time. I know and you know you can't pick an impartial jury in this county. Hell." Casey spat out the word. "If you do get a man on the jury panel with some sense, the ability to think, that prosecutor will use his—what did you call it? Peremptory challenge?—to yank him off. All we're gonna get on the jury is a bunch of jackasses that came to this country looking for something for nothing, expecting to find a Garden of Eden, and when they didn't find it they looked at me and my wife, the wealthiest folks in the county, and they felt cheated. They think it's our fault."

Amos P. Sharp was astonished at Casey's outburst, and he didn't know what to say. Casey went on.

"I feel sorry for their kids and women, and I'll feed them. My late wife has fed them. But those stump-headed men can go to hell."

"I understand how you feel. Unfortunately, everyone knows how you feel. That doesn't help."

Casey had spoken his mind on that subject, and he shut up. The lawyer was silent a moment, then went on with the business at hand.

"No date has been set for the new trial. I asked the judge to set bond. The prosecutor is opposed to it. Judge Buckley will rule on that tomorrow."

"I hope you can make him understand that I'm in danger of losing my property. Not only that, but somebody killed Reverend Weems, and I can't find out who if I'm locked up in jail."

"I know a very good private investigator you could retain."

"If I don't get out of here, I might have to do that."

The Doty boy was doing fine. Ruth Ann was pleased. He was outside when she called to check on him. Standing in the yard, facing the sun, he tilted his head back and opened his mouth wide while she took a look. "You're practically well. Your color is good. Voice box still a little sore, though, huh?"

"Yes'm."

"Don't talk any more than you need to. Soon you'll

be yelling like a wild Indian. Know what I've got in this sack? I brought you some vegetables and a cured ham. It would spoil if Dr. Woodrow kept it. I want you to eat your share of this ham. Will you do that?"

"Yes'm."

Walking back to the clinic, Ruth Ann reached a decision. Dr. Woodrow kept medical records of all his patients in file folders. There was a folder she wanted to look at. She could wait until the doctor was out attending to a house-bound patient, then have a look. But that would be sneaky. She wouldn't be sneaky. First, she'd ask the doctor, and if he couldn't remember what she wanted to know, she'd just simply look at the files. If he didn't approve, he could say so.

The doctor was in—sitting at his desk, filling out orders for medical supplies. When Ruth Ann arrived, he said, "Look and see how much mercuric chloride we have, will you? And check on the laudanum and the bromide. Perhaps we need more arnica and calomel. I know we need more cotton dressing. Sometimes I fail to order something I should order. Help me determine what we need, will you?"

Ruth Ann knew what they needed. She didn't have it written down, but she had it in her head. "I can fill out those orders, Doctor. I can figure out how to do it."

Looking up at her, he smiled. "Why, I believe you can at that. Would you please?" He stood and offered her his chair. "And, Ruth Ann, when there's a patient present, call me Doctor. But when we're alone, call me Ben."

She grinned a playful grin. "Sure thing, Benny Boy."

"Well," he laughed, "perhaps not Benny Boy." Still laughing, he added, "At least not in public."

It took two hours. No wonder the doctor never had any time for himself. When it was finished she asked him the question that was on her mind. He couldn't remember. She opened the file drawer in his desk and picked out the folder she wanted. The information was there, right at the top of the page.

"Well, now," Ruth Ann said, "this is getting curiouser and curiouser."

Chapter Twenty-Six

The drunk named Howdy finally quit snoring. His eyes opened, squinty at first, then wide. He sat up suddenly, cast a wild look around, then let out a long sigh of resignation. "Locked up again. Seems like I cain't get a few dollars' wages in my pockets 'thout gettin' likkered up and locked up."

Casey had other things on his mind, and he said nothing.

"Wonder what I done? Wonder if I hit somebody." He stood, walked to the cell door, looked out at the connecting door, sat again. "Last I recomember I was histin' a few at the Prospectors Saloon. Got fired. Boss said he couldn't pay me no more." He looked across at Casey. "Say, ain't you ... yeah, I recomember now, you're that Jim Casey feller."

"Uh-huh." Casey wondered if the man named Howdy would start a fight.

But Howdy wasn't in a fighting mood. "Yeah, I heered tell you was back in the hoosegow. Some a them fellers at the saloon said you was right where you belong. One or two said they wasn't so sure. Maybe it was only one that said that."

"Do you know his name?"

"Naw. Din't know nobody. The feller, whosomever he was, he said that preacher was a pussy hound."

"Huh?" Casey was listening carefully now.

"Thas what he said. Said he'd stick his diddly in anything that'd hold still. 'Nother feller tol' 'im to esplain that and he couldn't. Said thas what he heered somewheres."

"I wish you could remember that gentleman's name. Didn't somebody call him by name?"

"Not that I c'n recomember. Jist whiskey talk anyways. My boss and his wife, now they're teetotalers. They'd ruther eat shit than drink whiskey. And they wouldn't say shit if'n they had a mouthful. They thought that there preacher feller was . . . what she said oncet was 'he's a gift from heaven.' Me, I never set foot in his church."

"Didn't your boss try to get you to go to church?"

"Naw. I was jist a goddam hired man. I didn't count nohow. A goddam farmhand don't count for nothin' no time, no way, nohow."

For the second time in two days the news was good and bad. Amos P. Sharp told Casey the good news first. "The judge agreed to a bail bond. It took some arguing. The prosecutor pointed out the fact that you had escaped jail once. I argued that you turned yourself in, and that you are the biggest property owner in the county. I said you are extremely unlikely to abandon your property and become a fugitive for the rest of your life."

"Good, good," Casey said. "Let's post bond and get me out of here."

"The bad news is the judge is insisting on a property bond and you will have to tie up all your holdings."

"Everything?"

"Everything that is not already under mortgage."

"Why, this means . . ." Casey shook his head while the implications sunk in. "Does this mean I can't sell cattle to pay off a bank note?"

"I'm afraid it does."

"This is crazy. Nobody ever had to post that much bond."

Shrugging, the lawyer said, "I did the best I could. But look here, Mr. Casey, this does not mean you will lose your property. If you show up in court at the appointed times, the bond will be returned."

"Yeah, but . . ." Head down, Casey walked to the opposite end of the cell and back. "What about my account at the Farmers State Bank?"

"That will be attached also."

"Goddamn. I have to have some spending money."

"I'm sorry. I wish I could have done better. I tried. I did the best I could. The fact that you once escaped custody made it difficult."

Casey paced the cell again, deep in thought. His cell mate, Howdy, sat on his bunk and listened, but kept quiet. Then Casey said, "All right. The way I see it is if I don't get out of here, I'll probably lose everything anyway. If I'm free, maybe I can . . . I don't know what. Do something."

"I'll proceed to draw up the papers. I'll have to go to the county clerk to get a legal description of your real estate, and I will have to write the paper myself instead of dictating it. This will take some time, but by tomorrow morning at the latest I will have you out of here."

Glumly, Casey said, "Sure, sure."

Dr. Woodrow came, examined Casey's wound, and said it was healing nicely, but advised him to do nothing strenuous for some time yet. Mrs. Carter brought a beef stew. She'd marinated the meat until it was tender and tasty. Casey shared it with Howdy.

Next morning, he walked out of the jail.

Sheriff Waltham Jackson refused to give him his gun. "Orders from the judge. You're not to carry a weapon while you're out on bond. If I see you with a gun I'm s'posed to lock you up again."

That didn't worry Casey. He had more guns at the ranch house. What did worry him was the lack of money. He didn't feel well enough to ride a horse back and forth from the ranch house, and he had no money to rent a hotel room or eat at the cafe. His first stop— after blinking in the sunlight until his eyes quit watering—was the bank.

The citizens of Rockledge stared as Casey walked, slowly, with a little discomfort, across First Street and down the street a half-block to the Farmers State Bank. Bank President Shipley greeted him with a smile and invited him into his inner sanctum where they sat on opposite sides of a big oak desk.

"Yes," Shipley said somberly in answer to Casey's question, "your account has been attached."

"Well, that leaves me in a pickle."

The banker put his elbows on the desktop and made a steeple of his fingertips. "Mr. Casey, unsecured loans are considered very risky in banking circles. It is considered a bad practice." He pursed his lips. Casey knew he had more to say, and he waited. "Your account in this establishment, your business here, has at times enabled us to stay in business."

Again he paused. Casey waited.

The banker put his hands flat on the desk and said, "You can write checks on this bank anytime. You can write as many as you want and for any amount you want. The judge can order your account attached, but your checks will still be as good as gold."

For a moment, Casey was too surprised to speak. Finally, he said, "You'd do this for me?"

"Yessir, I will. Call it an unsecured loan, call it anything. You need some immediate cash funds, do you not? Here." The banker opened a desk drawer, took out a check book, and shoved it across the desk. "You write it and sign it and I'll cash it."

The incision in Mrs. Agnes Mooreman's stomach was healing, but too slowly. Dr. Woodrow wasn't pleased. "I expected to remove the sutures tomorrow," he told Ruth Ann after getting back to the clinic. "It's just not healing as fast as it should."

"But it is improving?"

"Yes, but I wonder why it's not improving at a more rapid rate. Stomach surgery is always very serious, very risky, but she seemed to be recovering. I was proud of myself. Now I'm a little worried."

"Is she in pain?"

"There is some pain, yes. Not severe, but enough that she is taking more laudanum than she should. Too much could be harmful."

"What can we do?"

"I'll have to find time to visit her every day until there is a definite improvement. I'm certain I took out every trace of the tumor, and I saw no evidence of a malignancy, but there is so much we don't know. I might have to open her up again."

"Oh, I hope not. The poor woman has suffered enough."

Sitting slumped at the desk, Dr. Woodrow sighed and shook his head. "There's so much we don't know."

Jim Casey didn't have to ride a horse back to the C Bar headquarters. His cook and housekeeper came to town in the one-horse buggy, bringing a basket of hot food. When Casey saw the rig in front of the sheriff's office, he crossed the street again.

"Oh, there you are," Mrs. Carter said. "I didn't know whether you was out or not. I brought you something to eat."

"I'll ride back with you," Casey said, "but don't worry, that chuck won't be wasted. There's another prisoner in there, and he doesn't like the cafe chuck any better than I do."

While they were in the sheriff's office, handing him the basket, Casey asked, "How long are you gonna keep him?"

"I'm taking him to the Justice of the Peace in about an hour. I know what the fine'll be. Ten dollars. He ain't got ten dollars, and the county can't afford to keep him locked up and feed him." Grinning at Mrs. Carter, he added, "What we need is more of your good grub, Mrs. Carter."

"Here." Casey said, taking a roll of bills from his shirt pocket and peeling off two fives. "Pay his fine and let him go."

The sheriff eyed the roll of money, but said nothing.

At the ranch house, Casey had to admit that moving hurt a little. Not much, but a little. And he promised not to move any more than he had to. In another day, Levi was back.

"Got a buyer comin' down tomorra. He's bringin' his saddle and bed, and I'm gonna meet 'im at Jack's Corners with another saddle horse and a pack horse. We're gonna look at all the cattle we can find, and it'll take two or three days. Hope we got some groceries left."

Happy that she didn't have to stay at the ranch alone, Mrs. Carter was cheerful. "You name it and we've got it."

Casey sat at the kitchen table with Levi and watched him sip hot coffee. He hated to say what he had to say. "Levi, uh, something else has come up. I, uh, had to put all my property, cattle and all, under bond to get out of jail."

The old man put his coffee cup down slowly, absorbing what his employer had said. "Does this . . . you can't sell no cattle?"

"No. Not until this whole mess is resolved."

"Oh my," Mrs. Carter said.

"Well, goshdurn it." Levi wouldn't swear in the presence of women or kids, but he had to express his feelings. "What're we gonna do?"

"I think," Casey said, "we ought to go on with what we've started. Let the cattle buyer look at the cattle and make an offer. Maybe I'll get lucky and find out who killed Reverend Weems and this mess will be over. If not, I'll have to tell the buyer we can't do business at this time."

A roast was cooking in the big Grand Windsor range, and potatoes were boiling on top. The smell of good food had spread throughout the ranch house. But it all was forgotten for the moment. Everyone was silent. Finally, Casey said, "I've got credit at the mercantile, and the bank will cash any checks I write. Let's just go on and see what happens."

"Well, uh, Jim, I already bought five horses and hired two cowboys. I spent some of the cash you gave me."

"You did what I asked you to."

"Yeah, I bought the horses off'n a cow outfit from

over west somewheres. They shipped a herd of beefs at the stockyards and didn't wanta take their remuda back with 'em."

"Good."

"And I . . . you might not like the two men I hired."

"I gave you authority to use your own judgment. That's all I can ask for."

"Buzz and Arnold." Levi added quickly, "They been ridin' for the Iliff outfit up north of Denver, and they didn't like it, and they quit and was hangin' around Denver lookin' for a job. They quit you when you needed 'em, but they're honest and they know the country around here, and I thought, uh . . ."

"I have no hard feelings. Buzz and Arnold are good men. Are they bringing the horses you bought?"

"Yeah. They'll be here late tomorra or the next day, ridin' two of the horses and leadin' three."

"I'll send them down south to help you and the buyer. When that job is done, they can go back to Hatchet Lake."

"Them cows're gonna start driftin' down purty soon. Somebody has to point 'em in the right direction and see they don't go over the divide. Buzz and Arnold know what to do."

"What I have to do, while you're gathering cattle and dickering with a buyer, Levi, is find out who killed that preacher. I can't get on a horse and help with the work just yet anyhow. If I can't figure out who the real killer is, then everything, no matter what we do, is all for nothing."

Chapter Twenty-Seven

He rode into town in the one-horse buggy, then got out in front of the hotel and handed the lines to Mrs. Carter. "I'll get a room here and if anybody needs to see me I'll be somewhere around here."

"Take care of yourself, Mr. Casey. Don't move too much. I'll come back to town in a day or two to be sure you're all right."

"Don't worry about me. Be handy in case Levi and his crew come to headquarters and need a feed."

If he hadn't already known he wasn't the most popular man in town, he would have known it now from the scowls he was getting. Hell with them, he thought. But the hotel clerk was friendly. "How do you do, Mr. Casey. You're gonna stay with us a while, huh? I'll give you one of our best rooms." He was a young man with a trimmed beard and thick dark hair parted in the middle.

"I don't suppose the lawyer, Amos Sharp, is here?"

"No. He keeps a room here, however, and he could be back any time."

"Well, it doesn't matter today."

The room held only the necessities; a narrow bed on springs covered with a brown blanket, a dresser with an oval mirror, a wash basin, a pitcher of water and a chamber pot under the bed. Casey had packed a small leather satchel with his razor, strop and soap, and one change of clothes. He left it on the bed without unpacking and went looking for the sheriff.

The sheriff wasn't in, and the door to his office was locked. Next, he went to the Howell Mercantile, got Tudor Howell off to one side, and asked, "Do you hear anything that might help me, Tudor? Somebody killed Reverend Weems and somebody else either knows about it or suspects something. Most folks can't keep their mouths shut forever."

"No, Jim. All I hear is what a shame it is that the reverend is dead. In fact, I'm sorry to say, what I hear is that you ought to be locked up. A couple of ladies in here just a while ago said if you weren't rich you would be." The merchant added quickly, "I'm on your side, Jim. I don't think you done it. If I can help you, holler."

Glumly, Casey said, "I wish you'd been on the jury." He looked around at the other customers, two women and a man. They were looking at him. The women were standing on the other side of a long wooden counter piled high with men's cotton and wool pants, shirts, and socks. Half the big room was stocked with clothes and the other half with groceries. One corner was divided with a portable wall. A hand-painted sign on the wall read: LADIES ONLY. In another corner was Hiram Samuels's pharmacy.

"I'm gonna start asking, Jim. I'm gonna start just point-blank asking folks who might have done it. Who knows, maybe somebody'll spill something."

Speaking low, Casey said, "I heard a rumor that the preacher liked the ladies maybe a little more than he should have."

"I sorta got that suspicion myself. In fact that Agnes

Mooreman, the one that testified against you, I hear that her and the reverend were spending a lot of time together."

"There's that. I think that's an established fact, but I don't know what to do with it."

"Maybe you oughtta hire one of them Pinkertons, Jim. They know how to ferret out information."

"Maybe I ought to. Maybe I will."

Sheriff Jackson still wasn't in, but Casey saw him coming. "Mornin', Jim," the sheriff said, walking up.

"Morning, Sheriff. Like to talk to you a minute."

Unlocking the door with a long key, the sheriff said, "Come on in."

Casey waited until they were seated, the sheriff in his desk chair, Casey in one of the other two chairs, then he said, "We know now that the shot that killed Reverend Weems came from a black powder gun. The cartridges my gun shoots will smoke a little and there might be a flash that you can see in the dark, but it wouldn't burn anything."

Nodding, Jackson agreed.

"Trouble is, almost everybody carries a black powder gun. There are more of them around than anything else."

"That don't narrow it down much, does it."

"The gun you're packing looks to be the double-action kind, and it no doubt shoots metal cartridges, too."

Another nod.

"What kind of gun does Deputy Rankin carry?"

"He packs a Remington .44 center fire."

"I never suspected him, anyway." Casey stood. "Well, it's something to keep in mind." He turned as if to leave, then stopped. "I hear, Sheriff, that the reverend liked the ladies. Have you heard any rumors like that?"

"Are you thinking maybe a jealous husband killed him?"

"I wouldn't rule it out."

"Rumor has it that Agnes Mooreman was spending a lot of time with him, but her husband died two years ago." Jackson grinned wryly. "He sure didn't do it."

"I knew Whit Mooreman. He was the kind that would shoot if he caught his wife with another man. But like you said, he's dead."

"If I knew of a suspect or anybody that was even a little bit suspicious I'd question him."

Casey shrugged. "I don't know any suspects."

Casey had promised Dr. Woodrow he'd go to the clinic and have his wound examined, and he turned his steps in that direction. Walking was a little uncomfortable, but bearable. Pedestrians he passed recognized him. Some scowled, some merely gawked. In spite of his discomfort, he held himself erect and walked proudly.

The doctor wasn't in, but his pretty assistant was. She was all professional. "Just lie here, Mr. Casey." She patted the examination table.

"Well, uh, when will the doctor be back?" He didn't want to be examined by a pretty young woman.

"Not until the middle of the afternoon. He had to visit a patient who lives about ten miles north of town." Ruth Ann smiled. "He said before he left that he certainly appreciates the horse you gave him. He calls the horse Redwing. It makes riding that far a pleasure."

"Well, uh, maybe I ought to come back later."

"I can save you a trip. If you will just lie down here. You don't have to take off your shirt, just pull up your shirttail."

"Well, uh . . ." He didn't want to, but he could think of no excuse. Reluctantly, he sat on the table, then lay back.

"Now let's see how you're doing?" She started pulling up his shirttail. He grabbed her hands. "Mr. Casey, please." He let go of her hands and pulled his shirttail up himself. She bent over him.

The doctor's assistant was a very pretty young woman. Young, fresh, cheerful. It made his heart ache. He remembered when Boots was young and fresh and beautiful. She'd grown older while they were building their ranch, acquiring land and cattle, but she was still beautiful and cheerful.

Ruth Ann straightened up, smiling. "I see no problem whatsoever. How do you feel?"

"Fine."

She turned serious. "It isn't healed yet, you know. The doctor used cat sinew to stitch the colon, and body heat will cause it to decompose in time. Until then you will continue to feel some discomfort. Please don't ride a horse for a while."

"I'm not planning to." Casey stood and tried to push his shirttail back inside his pants. It would have been easy if he could have unbuttoned his pants, but he couldn't do that in her presence. He did the best he could anyway.

"Mr. Casey, there's something you might find curious. You understand that I can't tell you what I'm told by the patients. But . . ."

Casey quickly forgot his embarrassment. He waited for her to go on.

"Let me mention a name. Jennifer Rankin."

"Who is she?"

"Deputy Rankin's wife."

Puzzled, Casey stammered, "Well, what . . . is she, uh . . . ?"

"I'm not giving away any confidences by telling you this. It's common knowledge around town, but perhaps you're not aware of it."

"What? Uh . . . ?"

"She suffered a cut lip and a broken forearm on the day the Reverend Weems was murdered. In fact, she walked in here about an hour before the fatal shot was fired. Dr. Woodrow keeps careful records, and he noted the day and the time of day that she came in."

Casey was silent while he mulled that over.

"I don't know whether it's important. Probably, it's not. I just thought you might like to know."

"I appreciate it, Miss Abraham. And you're right. It is curious."

Chapter Twenty-Eight

So a woman suffers a cut lip and a broken arm the same day Reverend Weems is killed. Is there a connection?

Miss Abraham must suspect there is, otherwise she wouldn't mention it. Frowning at the ground as he walked back to the hotel, Casey ran it through his mind. He'd learned two things about the reverend. No, make it two possible things. The reverend liked women. And he was a slick talker. He could make anybody believe anything. He could talk a woman into his bed. He didn't have to go to the women, they went to him to talk about religion, the Bible, and stuff like that. He was such a smooth jasper he could turn the subject around to whatever he wanted to turn it to. He'd probably persuaded Mrs. Mooreman to climb into his bed.

Casey remembered that the front door to the rectory, as they called the reverend's house, was unlocked. But there was a kitchen and there was an inner door that was shut. Well, so what? No matter how welcome his flock was, he had to have some privacy. He couldn't have people walking in while he was taking a bath or shaving.

The Reverend Weems had been a fairly young man,

about thirty-five. And, Casey reckoned, fairly handsome. Although Casey never could figure out what kind of looks women liked in a man.

Did the reverend bed down Jennifer Rankin, too? He'd have to be a bold son of a bitch to do that. Her husband was a deputy sheriff who kept no regular hours, could come home unexpectedly, and who always carried a gun. Not the kind of man the reverend would want to tangle with.

If they did it, they didn't do it at her house. They didn't need to. Mrs. Rankin could be seen going into the rectory every day and nobody would get suspicious. Except maybe her husband.

Casey decided he wanted to get a look at this Jennifer Rankin. How to do it? Just go up to the house and knock on the door? What would he say? That he was looking for the deputy? What if the deputy was at home and answered his knock?

Well, he'd stop at the sheriff's office and see if Deputy Rankin was there. If he was he'd—do what? Go to the Rankin house and make an ass of himself? And where was their house? Casey wished he'd asked Miss Abraham. Who could he ask?

Tudor Howell. Get him aside and ask him. Yeah, that's what he'd do.

The mercantile was busy. Casey counted five women and two men in the store for Howell and one clerk to wait on. The women were all middle-aged or older, plain, not the kind a younger man would want to sneak under the blankets with. The two men were looking at a Winchester repeating rifle, working the lever, sighting down the barrel. Howell glanced at Casey, but was too busy to say anything. Casey waited, ignoring the scowls from the women.

Eventually Howell managed to look Casey's way, and

Casey nodded toward a far end of the room. The two men met there, and Casey wasted no time. "Where does the deputy sheriff live? And do you know anything interesting about his wife?"

Howell answered just as fast, "A clapboard shack with a big rock chimney on the southwest corner three blocks north and a block west. His wife?" The merchant's forehead wrinkled in thought. "She's a pretty one. Next to the doctor's assistant, she's the prettiest woman in town. 'Course she wouldn't flirt with an old bat like me, but she's got wandering eyes. She knows she's pretty, and she likes having men slobber all over themselves at the sight of her. Why? Think she might have been one of the reverend's harem?"

Shrugging, Casey said, "I don't know. Somebody dropped her name. I'm curious, is all."

The sheriff was out, the deputy was in. "Don't know where he went," Deputy Rankin said. "Doesn't always tell me. Hell, he might be at home takin' a nap, for all I know."

"A nap?"

"Yeah, we got a saloon fighter locked up, and the sheriff had to stick around most of the night."

Just to make conversation, Casey asked "Since when do you lock up saloon fighters? Your jail ain't big enough to hold all of them."

"This 'un used a frog sticker. Cut a gash in a man's face. Had to get the doctor out of bed to sew 'im up."

"Oh. Well, I'll catch the sheriff later. It's not important."

Finding the house was easy. It had lacy curtains in the windows and flower boxes with red and yellow flowers under the two front windows. A small porch with one step up. Casey knocked on the door and tried to think of something to say.

She had flour on her hands and was wiping her hands on a short white apron. Her dark hair was done up in a knot behind her head. She was slender, shapely, pretty. Wide brown eyes were friendly at first. Then she recognized him.

Embarrassed, Casey stammered, "Excuse me, Mrs. Rankin, I was just, uh, I'm talking to some of the folks who knew Reverend Weems, and uh . . ."

"You're Jim Casey." It was an accusation.

"Yes, ma'am. I'm trying to find out who shot the reverend, and asking everybody I can if they know or suspect anything."

"You shot the reverend. You killed one of the finest men who ever lived in Rockledge. You're a land grabber and a greedy, selfish man."

"I didn't shoot him. I'm trying to find out who did. And I'm not a land grabber. I—"

He didn't get a chance to say more. She slammed the door.

A man without a horse could do a lot of walking, just getting around town. Casey judged from the sun it was about noon, and he walked to the cafe. He sat at one end of the counter, next to a burly gent in baggy bib overalls. Neither man spoke while Casey ate boiled cabbage, beans, and tough beef. Then, with nothing else to do, he walked to the rectory.

It was four rooms behind the church. Whitewashed like the church, but without a steeple. The door was unlocked, so Casey stepped inside. The room was immaculate. One of the women, or several women, no doubt kept it that way. There were a half-dozen wooden, straight-backed chairs, a stuffed sofa, and a stuffed chair. A cross was mounted on the walls at either end of the room, and a large copy of a painting of Jesus hung on another wall. An end table held a wood carving of two hands together in a praying position. The wooden floor was covered in the center with a hand-braided rug.

Standing in the spot where he'd stood about two months ago, Casey could picture in his mind the reverend in the center of the room, hate spewing out of his mouth.

"You're a sinner. You're a disciple of the devil. You have Satan in your soul."

And Mrs. Mooreman over by the sofa, mouth open, fear on her face.

The kitchen door was open then, and so was the bedroom door. Casey could remember seeing a bed covered with a multicolored patchwork quilt.

Out of curiosity, Casey went into the bedroom, saw nothing interesting, just men's clothes hanging from a wire stretched across a far corner. Leaving the bedroom, Casey wandered into the kitchen, and found that the door to another room opened from one side of the kitchen. He wandered into that room. It was another bedroom. Nothing unusual there. A bed with another handmade quilt. An armoire, a dresser. A chamber pot under the bed. Everything neat and clean.

As he stepped back into the kitchen, Casey realized that the door to the second bedroom couldn't be seen from the front room. A visitor in the front room wouldn't see the reverend coming from the second bedroom, not until the reverend got into the kitchen.

A good place for some secret lovemaking.

As he left the rectory, Casey met two middle-aged women coming in his direction. He guessed from the way their dresses fit that both were wearing tight corsets with bustles in the back. They had silly little hats pinned to their hair. They stared, then they frowned. Casey tipped his hat, and smiled a weak smile.

"Harrumph."

Feeling a little pain in his side and not knowing what else to do, Casey went up to his hotel room, pulled off his boots, and lay on the bed with his hands under his head. The ceiling was tin, designed with stamped-in squares. Idly, he started counting the squares, then suddenly realized what he was doing.

Forget that stuff, he told himself, and concentrate on your trouble. Think. What else can I do to solve this puzzle? He tried, but he could think of nothing else. All right, what have I learned? Let's see. Reverend Weems liked the ladies. He was almost certainly bedding the widow Mooreman. She thought they had something beautiful going. But when she was faced with serious surgery, she did a lot of praying. A guilty conscience? She must have felt some guilt. The church-going women believed that getting in bed with a man without marriage was a sin. Even when the man was a man of God. Even though both were single.

The reverend convinced her it was no sin, but somewhere in the back of her mind she felt a twinge of guilt.

So what?

It was the sheriff who first mentioned the possibility of a jealous husband being the killer. The more Casey thought about it the stronger the possibility became. Nobody else had a reason to kill the reverend. That's what made Casey look so guilty. Nobody else had a reason.

All right, it was a jealous husband. Who?

A man who had a beautiful wife like Jennifer Rankin and who was the jealous kind could be dangerous. Especially if the wife was a flirt. Tudor Howell said she had roving eyes and liked being admired. She was the kind that would drive a jealous husband crazy.

Deputy Rankin a killer? Could be. If he couldn't kill a man he wouldn't be a lawman. He wore the same kind of hat Casey wore. He was about the same size. The man seen running from the rectory that night could have been the deputy. The trial witness couldn't say for sure that it was Casey he saw, just that he saw a man who could have been Casey.

And the deputy's wife suffered a cut on the lip and a broken arm shortly before the fatal shot was fired. Did he get jealous and bust her one in the mouth?

Yep. In Casey's mind, Deputy Rankin was a prime suspect. But how to prove it? His wife would know. Or at least be suspicious. But she wouldn't talk.

Maybe the sheriff could get it out of her. If he tried. Maybe he wouldn't try. Maybe he would.

Casey swung his feet off the bed and sat up. Lying here was getting him nowhere. He could at least tell the sheriff about his suspicion. He pulled his boots on, ran his fingers through his hair, put his hat on, and went out on the street.

The sheriff wasn't in. The deputy wasn't in. Casey asked a pedestrian where the sheriff lived. The pedestrian spat a stream of tobacco juice into the street, wiped his mouth with the back of his left hand, and squinted at him.

"You're that Casey feller?"

"I'm Jim Casey."

"I oughtn' tell you anything."

"Why?"

" 'Cuz my woman cried for two days when that preacher was shot."

"Aw for . . ." This was getting damned exasperating. In fact, it was getting downright shitty. "Goddamit, you'd think that preacher was God almighty himself. I

214

didn't shoot the son of a bitch, but I'm glad somebody did."

The man was carrying a six-gun in a worn holster. Casey was not armed. But Casey said anyway, "The hell with you, mister." He turned his back on the man.

The next man he saw was Deputy Rankin, walking toward him. He waited, wanting to ask the deputy where the sheriff was. He didn't get a chance.

"I wanta talk with you." Rankin's eyebrows were pinched together and his mouth was tight. "I wanta talk with you right now. Get your ass in that office."

No doubt the deputy had just come from his house. His wife had told him about Casey's visit. Casey felt the way he felt when he was getting on a horse that was going to buck, was going to try to drive his head into the ground. Oh boy, he said to himself, here we go.

Chapter Twenty-Nine

Deputy Rankin didn't sit, didn't invite Casey to sit. He stood spraddle-legged, hands on hips. "Why in hell did you bother my wife?"

Before Casey could say anything, he went on, "I don't give a good goddam what kind of trouble you got, you leave my wife alone. Hear? She didn't have nothin' to do with nothin', and I won't stand for you or anybody else botherin' her. Hear?"

"I hear."

"Get your ass outta here before I lock you up again. And if you even look at my wife again I'll shoot the shit outta you. Hear?" The deputy's hand hovered over the gun on his hip.

No use trying to explain. This man wasn't going to listen to reason. No use saying anything. Casey left.

Outside, he was more suspicious of the deputy than ever. He was the kind that would fly into a jealous rage over his wife. But there was one thing about him that didn't fit. The reverend was shot with a black powder gun. And while the deputy was bawling him out, Casey noticed the gun he was carrying, and was reminded that Rankin's gun was a Remington six-shooter loaded with center-fire metal cartridges.

Aw shit, he said to himself. Excuse me, Boots.

It was a sleepless night. Though the hotel bed was comfortable enough, he was warm, and his stomach wasn't empty, he slept very little. He got out of bed, stood in the dark in his shorts, looking out the window at the street. Deserted. A half-moon put out enough light that he could make out the buildings, the bank, the mercantile. Except for a barking dog somewhere, it was quiet. Even the saloons were quiet.

Huh, Casey snorted, even in the daylight there wasn't a hell of a lot going on in Rockledge. The town was dying an inch at a time. The railroad did it. The railroad was a godsend to some folks, but to the merchants of Rockledge it was the beginning of the end. At first, when folks heard a railroad was going to be built south out of Denver, they had hopes it would come through Rockledge. But it went straight south instead, and missed Rockledge by about fifteen miles.

A gent named Jack had built a general store, a barn, and a warehouse where two wagon roads crossed and where the railroad had erected a water tank. His business was doing fine. And more buildings had gone up at Castle Rock, another water stop. The railroad had built a side track and stock pens at Castle Rock, and the C Bar could ship cattle from there instead of driving them all the way to Denver. That helped the C Bar and other cattlemen along the Front Range.

But the railroad sure played hell with Rockledge. Living was better near the railroad, and the old settlements were being left to die.

In another thirty or forty years Rockledge would be a weed-grown piece of ground with only a few chimneys and crumbling rock walls still standing.

Huh, Casey snorted again, if I live to an old old age maybe I can buy it for seventy cents an acre. Maybe I won't want it. Hell, maybe I won't have the money to buy it. Maybe I won't have a pot to pee in. Maybe . . . aw shit. Excuse me, Boots.

Sheriff Jackson was gone again. Deputy Rankin was getting ready to leave. He gave Casey an angry glare, then said sourly, "Walt's gone up to Denver. The district attorney up there wants to lay down the law to all the county sheriffs, tell 'em how to do things the legal way."

"How long will he be gone?"

"Two, three days. Me, I gotta go up to the north end of the county and try to keep two farmers from killin' each other over a land boundary. I'll write 'em a summons to court and let 'em do their fightin' there."

"That's the way it's done nowadays."

"Yeah, well, you keep your nose out of other folks's business, hear? Don't go botherin' nobody or I'll do more than write you a summons."

"Listen." Casey stood with his thumbs hooked in his belt. "I'm trying to clear myself of a murder charge, and I'm going to ask questions of everybody that might know something." He added one more word with sarcasm: "Hear?"

"I locked you up before, and I can do it again."

"Maybe you ought to be listening to the district attorney."

After the deputy left, Casey realized he'd said something foolish. It was foolish to get into an argument with the deputy. In fact, it was foolish to get into an argument with anybody.

The pancakes he'd had for breakfast sat heavy in his stomach. The cook at the cafe couldn't mix pancake batter the way Mrs. Carter did. And the eggs had been fried as hard as latigo leather. Casey was wishing he'd skipped breakfast when he saw a somewhat familiar face coming toward him. The face had been half-covered with a beard the last time he'd seen it, and now it was clean-shaven, the lower half almost white compared to the sun-darkened nose and cheeks.

"Howdy, Mr. Casey."

For a couple of seconds, Casey felt like laughing. How do you say "Howdy" to a man named Howdy? Finally, he said, "Morning, Howdy. I'm glad to see you're sober."

"Yessir. I ain't teched a drop since I was throwed in jail. I ain't never been drinkin' when I was s'posed to be sober."

"Well, everybody needs to take a snort now and then. Stay sober." Casey started to walk around him.

"Uh, Mr. Casey, I wanta thank you fer payin' my fine. I sure do 'preciate it. I was wonderin' if . . . I got laid off 'cuz my boss din't have the money to pay me no more, not 'cuz of my work. I'm a good worker, and like I said, I never been drunk when I was s'posed to be doin' somethin' else, and I'm needin' a job, and I was wonderin' if you c'd use another hand."

"Well . . ."

"I ain't no cowboy, I'll admit to that right now, but I c'n do anything else, and I know there's a lot of work to do on a cow ranch that don't have nothin' to do with herdin' cows."

Casey had to think about it. Looking down at the plank sidewalk, rubbing the back of his neck, he mulled it over. The man was right, there was a lot of work that couldn't be done on a horse, and he did need a man at headquarters. But how would Mrs. Carter like being alone at the ranch with a stranger?

"I c'n handle a team as good as anybody, and I done some blacksmithin', and I c'n dig postholes and build

219

fence, and I ain't never harmed nobody in my life 'less they harmed me first."

"Where do you come from, Howdy?"

"Muzzouree. My woman died of the smallpox. I got the wanderlust and come out here."

"Well, trouble is, Howdy, I haven't got time right now to go out to the ranch and put you to work. If you're still around in a few days I might put you on."

"I shore would like to work for you, Mr. Casey."

"My reputation doesn't bother you?"

"Nossir, it don't. I don't know if you killed that preacher like some folks say you did, but I'm bettin' if you did you had a good reason."

"How are you fixed for eating money?"

"I'm down to my last twelve cents."

"Well, here." Casey took a roll of bills out of a shirt pocket and peeled off two ones. "This will keep the wrinkles out for a while. I can't promise you a job so don't pass up any opportunities. If you're still around the next time I go to the ranch, I might take you along."

A calloused hand took the money. "I shore do thank you, Mr. Casey. You c'n take this outta my wages." The man named Howdy moved on toward the cafe.

Now what? Casey stood on the street in front of the sheriff's office, trying to think of something. He'd like to have another talk with the doctor's assistant, Miss Abraham. She appeared to be a woman with a burning curiosity, and she might know something else that would help. But how to approach her? Just walk into the doctor's office? Naw. Tomorrow, maybe. He'd be due for another examination tomorrow. And then she probably wouldn't tell him any more than she'd already told him. Professional ethics. Besides, he wanted to do something now.

The woman he'd most like to ask questions of was

the widow Mooreman. She might have seen something or heard something. Forget that. She was convinced he'd killed the reverend, and she wouldn't tell him the way to a toilet.

Thinking, worrying, Casey saw three riders out of the corners of his eyes. They were coming down First Street, probably from some cow outfit over the divide. Casey paid them no attention. Then suddenly an image popped into his mind. The image of three would-be rustlers up in the mountains, driving a small bunch of stolen cattle. He had a recollection of gunfire.

He wanted to take a good look at them to be sure, but if he did they would recognize him. Casey turned his back to them. He took off his hat and scratched his head, pretending he had no interest in them whatsoever. He heard them ride past, slowly, leisurely.

If they were who Casey thought they were, they had no doubt looked him over. They'd looked over everybody in sight. He carried no gun, and apparently he didn't look like a threat. He listened, fighting down the temptation to turn his head and study them.

The hoofbeats stopped. Saddle leather creaked as somebody dismounted. From the sounds, he knew they were near the bank.

He had to look now. Had to be sure. Turning, Casey saw two men going into the bank. Their backs were to him, and he didn't recognize their backs. The one man outside had stayed on his horse, and was holding the other two horses by the bridle reins. Casey studied the man's face. He was no one he'd ever seen before.

But he was looking hard at Casey, wary, right hand near the gun on his hip.

For the first time in many years, Casey had no gun when he needed one. His Navy Colt was in the sheriff's office somewhere. He wasn't supposed to carry a weapon while he was waiting trial. Right now he needed a gun.

Turning suddenly, Casey grabbed the knob on the door to the sheriff's office, expecting the door to be locked. The knob turned. Surprised, Casey ducked inside, took a quick look through the small glass window, saw the one rider still there outside the bank. Then he started looking for a weapon.

A lever action rifle and a double-barreled shotgun were in an iron rack against the far wall, but the rack had a big padlock on it. Hastily, Casey started going through the sheriff's desk. He yanked open three drawers before he found a gun.

It was an old cap and ball, black powder Dragoon. Moving fast, Casey grabbed it, flipped open the loading gate, saw it was loaded and had percussion caps on the firing nipples. He cocked the hammer back, then took another look out the window.

They were running out of the bank, one carrying a tow sack, the bottom half bulging. He recognized them then. They were getting on their horses.

Casey stepped outside, yelled, "Halt. Stop or I'll shoot."

That was dumb. He should have fired first, then yelled. A shot was snapped his way. It crashed through the window behind him. He aimed at the man carrying the sack, but before he could squeeze the trigger a bullet hit him a staggering blow on the left shoulder. He fell back against the window, but stayed on his feet.

He aimed again, fired.

The old Dragoon belched fire and smoke. It also shot a heavy lead ball straight at the target. The man fell off his horse, dropping the sack. One of the others started to get down and pick up the sack, but more men were out in the street now, firing wildly.

Two men socked spurs to their horses and rode on a dead run down the street and out of town. Their partner stayed on the ground, not moving. The sack was at his side.

Someone yelled, "Where's the sheriff?" Another yelled, "They didn't get the money. The money's in that there sack."

Bank President Shipley staggered out of the bank, blood running out of a cut on his head. One of his clerks came out, too, with a pistol in his hand. Men were looking around wildly, ready to blaze away at anyone who resembled a bank robber.

Casey held the Dragoon down at his side. His left shoulder was numb. He walked over to the small crowd that had gathered around the downed robber. He tried to walk straight and strong, but he knew he was staggering a little. No one noticed him at first, then a man said, "He's the one that shot 'im. Shot 'im right out of his saddle."

Then Shipley noticed him. "Good God, Jim, did you . . . Judas Priest, you've been hit." Shipley picked up the bag and handed it to his clerk. "Put this back where it belongs." Then to Casey he said, "Let me see. How bad is it?" With blood running down his own face, the banker took a close look at Casey's bloody left shoulder. "Jim, you need a doctor." He turned to the crowd. "He saved the bank's money. Let's get him to the doctor."

Grinning a weak grin, Casey said, "You could use some doctoring yourself."

Chapter Thirty

"Mr. Casey, can you walk? Let me help you, Mr. Casey." It was Howdy, taking Casey's right arm and putting it over his shoulder. "If'n you cain't walk, we'll carry you."

"I can walk, Howdy.".

"I know where the doctor's house is. It ain't far. I'll help you, Mr. Casey."

Two men, one bleeding from a cut on the head and the other bleeding from a bullet wound in the shoulder, made their way on unsteady legs, hanging on to other men, to the clinic. While they walked, Shipley said, "That dead one, he's one of four hoodlums that tried to molest a young woman in the street a while back. Your man Levi shot one and the other three left town."

"I recognized two of them," Casey said. "Three men tried to steal some cattle up in the high country, and I shot one. I don't know whether he survived, but the other two had to recruit some help to try the bank."

They reached the door at the same time, but Shipley stepped back and allowed Casey to enter first. The doctor was in his kitchen, sterilizing his instruments. Ruth Ann saw them before he did, her eyes taking in the bloody face and the bloody shoulder.

"Doctor," she said loudly but calmly, "we need you out here immediately." She shooed the other men outside.

Feeling weak, Casey sat in one of the chairs in the examination room. Shipley sat in the other. Before the doctor came out of the kitchen, Ruth Ann had looked at the banker's wound, then turned to Casey and started unbuttoning his shirt."

"What happened?"

Shipley answered, "The bank was robbed. Jim there shot one of the robbers and we recovered the money."

"Oh my."

Not until then did Casey realize he was still carrying the Dragoon. He carefully placed it on the floor beside his chair.

Dr. Woodrow parted Shipley's hair with his fingers, murmured, "This will need some sutures," then went to Casey.

Ruth Ann asked, "Which one first, Doctor?"

In his professional voice, the doctor said, "Miss Abraham, will you shave the hair from around Mr. Shipley's wound? There is hot water in the kitchen. While you are doing that, I will examine Mr. Casey more thoroughly." He urged Casey to lie on the examination table, then finished removing the shirt, and probed with his fingers. "Can you move your arm, Mr. Casey?"

Casey managed to move his forearm, but when he tried to move his upper arm, pain shot through him, forcing a grunt.

After more probing, the doctor said, "The lead is still in there. We will have to go in. First, let me attend to Mr. Shipley."

While the banker sat stiffly in his chair, Ruth Ann carefully shaved a large spot on his head, then washed the wound. She also washed the blood off his face. "What hit you, Mr. Shipley?"

"A gun barrel. I didn't move fast enough for one of the robbers."

"Oh my."

It took six stitches to close the wound on the banker's head. That was covered with a white bandage. Shipley stood, looked down at his bloody shirt, and allowed, "I know I look awful, but I feel all right. I must return to the bank."

Ruth Ann said, "A cut on the head can bleed a lot and look worse than it is, but you really should go home and lie down, Mr. Shipley."

A half-dozen townsmen were outside, rehashing the robbery, exchanging stories about what each had seen, and waiting to find out how badly the two men were hurt. One asked, "Want I should get you a buggy, Mr. Shipley?"

Trying to look and act dignified, the banker said, "I don't believe that will be necessary. Thank you very much anyway."

Inside, Dr. Woodrow was preparing his chloroform inhaler. "Without this, Mr. Casey, the pain would be unbearable."

Mrs. Carter recognized Buzz and Arnold when they rode into the ranch yard, leading three horses. It was late afternoon, and when she went out to meet them, they said they'd left Denver about daylight that morning. She passed along the instructions Jim Casey had left for them. They were to go to Squaw Mountain, taking six horses with them, and find Levi and the cattle buyer. They were to help gather cattle from the higher hills west of Squaw Mountain, and push them down

226

onto the prairie. Levi was the boss until Jim Casey was back.

It would be dark long before they got to the Squaw Mountain camp, and no one expected them to leave that day. "I shore am anxious to wrap myself around some a your good cookin', Mizz Carter," Buzz said.

"Can we do anything for you?"

"I could use some firewood," Mrs. Carter said. "But I'm not the boss so I can't tell you what to do."

"I'll go to work on that right now, ma'am. Ol' Arnold here, he can jangle in the horses and rope out some fresh mounts."

The two cowboys had stayed at the C Bar headquarters before and they knew what to do. And Mrs. Carter was glad to have some company.

The ceiling swam when Jim Casey opened his eyes. He squinched them shut, then opened them again slowly. The ceiling was fuzzy now. Without moving his head, he sent his eyes roving over what he could see. The face off to his right was a woman's.

"Don't move yet, Mr. Casey. You'll feel better soon. Just lie still."

He mumbled something about how he was more than happy to just lie still. Ruth Ann smiled.

The next time he opened his eyes he could see a little better. He started to move, found his left shoulder too heavy, and relaxed again. Wondering why his shoulder was so heavy took too much brain power. Fuzziness returned.

A man's voice said, "His pulse is strong. His heartbeat is normal. He's coming out from under."

Casey made out Dr. Woodrow's face. His eyes rolled to his right, and he made out Ruth Ann. "Uhh. I guess

I'm still alive." He started to rise. A gentle hand held him down.

"Wait until your vision clears, then you can sit up." He lay still, rolling his eyes, trying to see his left shoulder without turning his head. All he saw was something white. Slowly, expecting pain, he turned his head and saw the bandage covering his entire shoulder, the top half of his chest, and his left arm.

"Well." He lips felt numb, and he swallowed a lump in his throat. Trying again, he managed, "You'd pass for an angel, miss, but if I ain't dead I'd better get up."

"Trying to keep you cowboys down is a job in itself, but here, let me help. Careful, careful."

His vision swam and a tom-tom was pounding in his head when he sat up. But gradually he got his eyes focused. "Whoo."

"If you feel faint, just lie back."

"I was shot again, wasn't I?"

Dr. Woodrow said, "Yes, but again you were fortunate. The bullet missed the scapula and the clavicle, but invaded the deltoid. Your left arm will be useless for a time."

"The what?"

Ruth Ann interpreted, "It missed your shoulder and collarbones, but tore the deltoid muscle."

"It will heal in time, but you may not have full strength in your left arm."

"Ohhh."

"Keep your arm in the sling and don't move it. Give it time."

"Then I won't have to stay in bed?"

"No, but you'll be weak. I don't want you walking so soon after chloroform. Just lie down and rest."

Sinking back on the examination table, Casey said, "I

hope nobody else needs this bed. I could sleep for a week."

"You're quite a hero," Ruth Ann said. "They say you saved the bank's cash, and quite a few folks around here are grateful."

Suddenly, Casey remembered the gun he'd used. "Say, the pistol I was carrying, is it still here?"

"Yes. It's on the floor over there where you left it."

"Don't let anybody take it."

"I won't."

It was nearly dark when he felt steady enough to walk. His shoulder was throbbing. Ruth Ann tried to button his bloody shirt around his chest, but finally had to cut the left sleeve and shoulder off to button it. Dr. Woodrow gave him some laudanum for the pain and some bromide to help him sleep.

He walked slowly, carefully, to his hotel room where he ruined a shirt, cutting it to fit. It was awkward work, cutting with a pocket knife while holding one end of the shirt on the floor with his foot and the other end with his teeth. But when he finished, he got the shirt on and buttoned most of the buttons. Looking at himself in the oval mirror, he grimaced, "Jim Casey," he said aloud, "you look like you've been shot at and missed, shit at and hit."

At the cafe, his arm in a sling, he sat at the counter and read the handwritten menu tacked to the wall. The wrinkled old woman who waited on customers at the counter was friendly for a change. "I'll fix you anything you want, Mr. Casey. Do you feel like some roast beef? We've got some mashed spuds and some water gravy that oughtta go down easy. I'll scramble you some eggs if you want."

Looking around, Casey realized the faces were no longer scowling. Instead they looked downright sociable. "Need any help with anything, Mr. Casey?" He didn't recognize the man. "No, but thanks anyway," Casey said. "Uh, my name is Jim."

"Sure, if you say so, Jim."

With only one useful hand, he had to cut the beef with a fork, but it was tender. In fact, this was the best meal he'd ever had in the Rockledge Cafe. In his room, he managed to get his boots off with one hand. He mixed some of the bromide in a half glass of water and drank it. Then he slept.

Mrs. Carter was horrified when she came to town in the one-horse buggy. "Poor Mr. Casey. That's twice you've been shot."

"It could be worse," he grinned. "I could be dead."

"Let me fix you another shirt. Can I buy one at the mercantile? I can get some thread and a needle and fix a shirt so it looks better."

"Aw, don't bother with that now, Mrs. Carter. Right now I need to send a telegraph up to Denver."

"Can you get in the buggy? I'll drive you over to the telegraph office."

The gun wasn't where he'd left it on the floor at the doctor's office, and for a moment Casey was worried. Then Ruth Ann fetched it from somewhere and handed it to him. "It's ugly," she said. "It's heavy and ugly. Is it the one you used to stop the robbery?"

"Yes. Uh, Miss Abraham, I, uh . . ." Casey had a question but he didn't know how to word it. "You mentioned Jennifer Rankin, and I, uh, I'm beginning to suspect she was somehow mixed up in the reverend's murder. Can you tell me any more about her?"

230

"Do you think she might have shot him?"

"No, not her, but . . ."

"Oh. I think I see what you're getting at. Well, I'm not violating any professional ethics when I tell you about the rumors I've heard at Mrs. Spencer's boardinghouse. I've heard that she is—not exactly what you could call flirtatious—but she does like to be seen. That's a rumor. And she does have moon eyes for the doctor. That's a fact."

"Uh-huh. Hmm. Moon eyes, means . . . ?"

"She flirts with him."

"Uh-huh." Well, Casey thought, that confirms what he'd already been told. Then he remembered something else he wanted to ask about. "Is the doctor in, Miss Abraham?"

"Yes. I'll call him." She turned her head and said, "Doctor, Mr. Casey would like to see you." Dr. Woodrow came from the office with a questioning look on his face. "Yes, Mr. Casey?"

"Uh, Doctor, I've got a question that has to do with the murder of Reverend Weems. Did you, when you determined the cause of death, take the bullet out of his body?"

"Why, no. I went in, but the missile was so badly splintered it would have taken a considerable amount of time. I thought it was pointless, since the victim had expired."

"I see. Thank you, Doctor."

Amos P. Sharp telegraphed back that he'd be down on the next train south, but that wouldn't be until the next morning. He'd take the stage from Jack's Corners as usual. Casey didn't want to see the deputy, and he didn't want to put the Dragoon back where he'd found it, not until he could show it to the lawyer and the sheriff. He went to the ranch house with Mrs. Carter, plan-

231

ning to be back to town early. While he tried his skill at chopping wood with one hand, Mrs. Carter cut and tailored two shirts so he could slip them under the sling and over his shoulder, and button them all the way.

In the morning, he was back in town, and was surprised to find Sheriff Jackson in his office. "I've got something to tell you," Casey said, "but I want the lawyer Amos Sharp to be here."

"I heard about the bank robbery, and how you shot one of the robbers out of his saddle. Seems folks have a little higher opinion of you now. They'd be hurting financially without that bank money. Say, where'd you get the gun?"

"Out of that drawer there."

Sheriff Jackson yanked open the desk drawer, then slammed it shut. "You took that old Colt's Dragoon. Where is it?"

"In my room at the hotel. That's one of the things I want to tell you and the lawyer about."

"Did you learn something about the reverend's murder?"

"Yeah. I don't know whether I can prove it, but I know who shot him."

Chapter Thirty-One

The four-up stage didn't have far to travel from Jack's Corners and was always on time. It carried only two passengers, which would have made it an unprofitable business had it not been for the U.S. mail contract. Jack himself was handling the driving lines. With his handlebar moustache, waxed and curled up on the ends, he seemed to be always smiling.

"Say," he drawled, "I hear tell there's been a lot of gunfire in this town. Jim, what happened to you?"

"I caught some of that gunfire," Casey said.

"Do tell. I gotta know more about this. Soon's I water these hosses." He clucked to the team, turned the coach around in the street, and headed off toward the freight pens.

To Amos P. Sharp, Casey said, "Still got that room in the hotel?"

"Yessir, I have." The lawyer was dressed in his usual natty fashion, with a stiff collar, cravat, and dark finger-length coat.

"Let's get the sheriff and go over there. I've got something to say, and we don't need any interruptions."

Sheriff Jackson went willingly, and within minutes the three men were in the lawyer's room with the door closed. Casey stood before them, rubbing his sore shoulder. The lawyer sat in the only chair the hotel furnished and the lawman leaned against a wall, waiting for him to speak.

"All right, here's what happened. You're not gonna like this, Sheriff, but I don't like being convicted of a murder I didn't commit."

They watched his face, waited.

"What happened is this. Reverend Weems liked the ladies. He liked to take them into his bedroom at the rectory. He took the widow Mooreman, and he took Jennifer Rankin, and maybe others."

Waltham Jackson's eyebrows went up and his mouth opened. Casey put up his one good hand and said, "Now hear me out."

Jackson's mouth closed.

"Your deputy, Sheriff, is married to a very pretty young woman. He knows she's a beauty, and so does she. He's the jealous kind. I've seen myself how he can fly into a rage over his wife. She's—nobody that I've talked to has accused her of outright flirting in public—but it's a known fact that she doesn't discourage men from trying to flirt with her."

"Are you saying my deputy shot that preacher?"

"Yessir, I am."

"Nossir. I don't believe it."

"Look at it this way: Weems smooth-talked her into his bedroom. Deputy Rankin got suspicious and went to check. He either caught them in the act, or about to commit the act, or right after the act. He busted his wife in the mouth, which split her lip. The blow knocked her down and broke her arm. While she was in the doctor's office getting her arm set, Rankin went home and brooded. The more he thought about it the madder he got. He decided to kill the reverend. You can figure out the rest, Sheriff."

Jackson paced the floor, pulling at his chin. He looked out the window for a moment, then turned back. "And you figure he used that old Colt's Dragoon. Why didn't he use his own gun?"

"His gun fires a bullet that's shaped different from a lead ball. He thought if he used the Dragoon, and the ball was dug out of the dead man and identified as the kind that's fired from a black powder gun, he wouldn't be suspected. But the ball was so shattered, the doctor couldn't—or didn't—dig out the pieces. The victim was dead, so why bother? If it hadn't been for the burns on the shirt, nobody would know what kind of gun fired the shot."

"Why didn't the doctor say something about the burned shirt when he was on the witness stand?"

Casey looked at Amos P. Sharp, then back to the sheriff. "I learned something during that trial. I learned how trials are conducted, and I can't say I like it. Witnesses are sometimes told to answer yes or no, then shut up. Dr. Woodrow tried to say something, but didn't get a chance."

"Naw, naw." Jackson was shaking his head. "Naw, I can't believe it."

"You know your deputy better than I do. Have you ever seen him get jealous, I mean mad jealous, over his wife?"

"Well, well . . ."

"And what would you do if you saw your wife on a bed with another man? Or coming out of the bedroom buttoning her clothes?"

"I'd prob'ly kill the son of a bitch, but . . . see here, you don't know that Mrs. Rankin ever went to bed with Reverend Weems."

235

"I'd bet on it. You do some checking. You'll believe it, too."

"Aw, naw." The sheriff was still shaking his head.

"Another thing. Breaking out of jail was too easy. Deputy Rankin was in the office, asleep, maybe, but not dead. I muffled the sound somewhat with some blankets, but it still should have woke him up. I knew it was easy, but I didn't know why—until now."

"You're saying he wanted you to bust out?"

"Yep. That put a double diamond hitch on the case. No matter what came out after that, nobody would ever suspect anybody but me."

"Huh-uh. Naw."

"You give it some thought. Remember the trial witness who said he saw a man running from the direction of the rectory? He couldn't say for sure it was me, only that it could have been me. Rankin is about my size and he wears a hat shaped like mine. It was him."

All Sheriff Jackson could do was pace the floor and shake his head.

Casey asked, "What do you think, Mr. Sharp?"

Until now, the lawyer had kept quiet. Now he scowled at the floor for a moment, then looked up. "You've talked about plenty of reason to suspect Deputy Rankin. I think it's something the sheriff should investigate. Perhaps question Mrs. Rankin."

"What do you think about that, Sheriff?"

"She wouldn't say a thing that would hurt her husband."

"Even though he knocked her down?"

"No. I'd have to pull some kind of trick on her, and I'm not very good at trickery."

"It will take expert interrogation," the lawyer said. "If necessary I will call her as a trial witness and have her put under oath. If she lies, she will be guilty of perjury."

All were silent a long moment. Casey sat on the bed and rubbed his shoulder. It throbbed painfully with every heartbeat. Jackson looked out the window at nothing in particular. Amos P. Sharp scowled at the floor.

Finally, the lawyer spoke, "I, uh, don't want to tell you how to do your job, Sheriff, but perhaps you should confront Deputy Rankin with what Mr. Casey said. Sit him down, just the two of you, and put it to him bluntly. See how he reacts."

"All right." Jackson sighed, raised his hands, let them drop. "If it'll make the two of you happy, I'll do that. But what if he denies everything?"

"Then," now the lawyer was shaking his head, "I don't think we have enough evidence to get the prosecutor to charge Deputy Rankin. We will need further evidence."

Chapter Thirty-Two

"She doesn't look good," Dr. Woodrow said, frowning at the desktop in his office. "She's in pain, and there's nothing I can do about it. Laudanum helps, but not enough. I'm afraid I'm going to have to open her up again and see what's happening."

"It sounds to me, Ben, like she's going to die anyway." Ruth Ann sighed. "I'm no doctor, but it seems to me that if she hasn't improved by now she isn't going to. I remember a rancher in Wyoming saying once that when a cow decides it's time to die nothing can save her. Perhaps Mrs. Mooreman is that way."

"I don't know. I mentioned the possibility of more surgery, and she took it calmly, as if she had expected it."

"When will you make a decision?"

"In a few days. I failed to take some fresh cotton cloth with me. I wish you would go over there, Ruth Ann, and change the bandage. Will you do that now?"

"Of course."

Amos P. Sharp agreed to stay in Rockledge a few days, and he wired the district attorney in Denver that new evidence had been discovered in the Reverend Weems murder case. The district attorney wired back that he needed more details before he would send a deputy DA down.

Sheriff Waltham Jackson did as the lawyer suggested and questioned his deputy closely. Not only did he learn nothing, but the deputy refused to allow his wife to be interrogated. Told that she could be subpoenaed and placed under oath, his reply was: "That's what you'll have to do."

The next telegram to the DA informed him that a hostile witness might have to be subpoenaed to get at the truth, and Amos P. Sharp would like to have a deputy DA present.

The DA still insisted on more details.

"That's where it stands," the lawyer explained to Casey. "If we could only place Deputy Rankin at the scene of the crime, or find a witness who will testify that the Reverend Weems was having an affair with Mrs. Rankin, we would have a much stronger case."

Casey went to Sheriff Jackson. "The widow Mooreman has all but said she was hopping into bed with the reverend. She has all but admitted she lied on the witness stand. I've got a hunch she knows more."

"What can I do?" The sheriff leaned back in his chair and spread his hands. "She's sick. If I went over there and interrogated her I'd look like the meanest son of a bitch in Colorado."

"I'll tell you one thing, Walt." Casey stood with his left arm in a sling and his right thumb hooked inside his waistband. "I didn't kill that preacher, and I've put up with all this horseshit long enough. I've got a cow outfit to run, and I'll be damned if I'm gonna just sit on my ass and wait for something to happen."

"What've you got in mind?"

"I don't know. I'll think of something."

"Now don't you go picking on folks. You stay away from Jennifer Rankin, and you stay away from Mrs. Mooreman. You go picking on a sick woman, and I'll have to arrest you for something or other."

"I'm gonna do whatever has to be done." Casey turned on his boot heels and walked out onto the street.

Restless, he walked up one side of First Street and down the other. He walked past the saloons, the blacksmith shop, the harness maker, the laundry, the bank, the mercantile. Deep in thought, he didn't see the other pedestrians on the street. Soon he found himself at the freight pens where some of the townspeople kept their horses and buggies. Now that the railroad had passed within fifteen miles of Rockledge, the freighting business had fallen off, and the new owner had a few more wagons than he needed. One of the high-sided freight wagons still had the name of the previous owner painted on its side: WHIT MOOREMAN'S STAGE AND FREIGHT LINE. DENVER TO ROCKLEDGE.

Whit Mooreman was a tough old bird. Casey could see him in his mind's eye toting an old Henry rifle and a hogleg six-gun on every trip. He'd fought off an attack by a small band of Arapahoes once with those guns. The Indians killed two of the four horses he'd had hitched to his wagon, but he'd killed two of the attackers. Yeah, old Whit was tough but honest. His widow now?

She'd changed her story a little in a statement to Amos Sharp. Would she change it further?

Casey went to the cafe for dinner. It was noon, and the cafe was crowded with working men, men without wives. Oh well, he was idle. He could wait. On the boardwalk, he stood in the shade of the building and tried to figure out a plan. Sheriff Jackson had said it

240

would take a mean son of a bitch to question the widow Mooreman. Maybe it would.

Maybe it wouldn't.

Either way, he wanted to question her. She probably knew the reverend better than anyone else. She'd spent a lot of time in the rectory. The chances were good that she'd seen or heard something that was important to a defendant in a murder trial. If she had she wasn't going to volunteer it. The Reverend Weems had called him a disciple of the devil, and she believed everything the reverend said. Whatever happened to Casey didn't worry her at all.

Well, by god, it worried him. He was the one who stood to lose everything, even his life. The sheriff wouldn't question her because he was a politician who wanted to be popular with the voters. Casey was no politician, and the damned town had dirtied on him anyway. Mean son of a bitch or not, he was going to question her. Decision reached, he turned and walked to her house.

But when he got there he didn't know what to do. If she was alone she couldn't answer his knock on the door. And he couldn't just walk in. He knocked anyway, waited. A woman's voice inside said to "Come in." Should he or shouldn't he? Then he noticed a woman next door watching him from a window. He went over and knocked on her door.

"Ma'am," he said when she opened the door, "I need to talk to Mrs. Mooreman a minute, and I wondered if you could . . ."

"You're Jim Casey." Another accusation.

"Yes, ma'am, I am." He waited for her to slam the door in his face, or scold him. She stood there, staring at him, not moving. Middle-aged, plump.

"I do need to talk to Mrs. Mooreman. I promise I

won't hurt her or question her if she's too sick to talk. I was wondering if you're a friend of hers."

"Yes, I am. I'm Mrs. Gibbons, and I've been taking care of her."

"That sure is good of you, Mrs. Gibbons. I was wondering if you would go with me, be with her, when I ask a couple of questions. It would sure help us both if you would."

Her eyes took in the left arm in a sling. "You're the one that stopped the bank robbery."

"I, uh . . ."

"And got shot. Well, you did save the bank's cash. All my money's in the bank. I guess I owe you something for that. Yes, I'll go with you. But only for a minute, you understand."

"I'd sure appreciate it."

The widow Mooreman was propped up on two fat feather pillows. Her eyes opened wide when she recognized Casey. She started to say something, then closed her mouth. Her neighbor spoke quickly, "Agnes, dear, this is the gentleman that saved the bank's cash and got hisself shot doin' it. Your money is in the bank, too, and I thought maybe you wouldn't mind if he asked you a question."

The widow Mooreman's voice was a little weak, but not much. "I can't help you, Mr. Casey."

Standing at the foot of her bed, Casey asked, "Would you mind trying? I mean, try to remember anything you saw or heard that might help me?"

"I didn't see or hear anything."

It was obvious she wasn't going to volunteer a damned thing. Being polite was getting Casey nowhere. He glanced at the neighbor woman, then said bluntly, "You were going to bed with the reverend. You went to the rectory and went to bed with him. This had been going on for quite a while."

Her mouth opened, shut, opened again. "No, that's not so. We . . ."

"It is so. Everybody knows it."

"No." Her voice was rising. "I . . . that's not so."

"Agnes," the neighbor said, "you don't have to put up with these questions." To Casey she said, "It's time you left now. You're getting her excited, and the doctor said she shouldn't get excited."

Casey said, "I apologize, but my life, everything I own, is depending on her honesty. She has to be honest about it."

The neighbor was looking from Mrs. Mooreman to Casey, back and forth.

Casey went on, "You thought he was a saint. Somehow he made you believe that what you were doing was all right."

While he talked, her expression went from one of annoyance to surprise to hurt. Now she blurted, "Yes. He said we were only doing what the almighty intended, and together we could do great and wonderful things."

"But then you found out he was a mortal just like the rest of us, and had the same wicked desires of the flesh. He was a sinner, wasn't he, Mrs. Mooreman? You saw him with Jennifer Rankin, didn't you?"

"No, no." She waggled her head from side to side on the pillows.

"You walked in and saw them, didn't you?" Louder, he repeated, "Didn't you?"

"He was . . ." Her face twisted in anguish. "He was sinning. With us it was beautiful. But he ruined it. He was an adulterer. He was . . ." Tears ran down her face, and she couldn't go on.

"One more question, Mrs. Mooreman. Did you see

243

Deputy Rankin at the rectory when Reverend Weems was shot?"

"No. I saw nobody. Yes, I saw a man running away. I don't know who."

"Thank you very much, Mrs. Mooreman. I wish you well."

She was crying uncontrollably now. Her neighbor gently wiped her tears with a linen handkerchief.

"I apologize to you both," Casey said. "I hope you understand why I did this."

Chapter Thirty-Three

Judge Harold J. Buckley had to travel to Rockledge and listen to two neighbors argue over a land boundary. He would much rather have stayed in the more comfortable city of Denver, but duty called. When the district attorney learned that the judge was going to Rockledge, he sent along the deputy DA who did the prosecuting in Oak County. He gave his deputy instructions to listen to any new evidence there might be in the Reverend Weems murder case. The prosecutor and Judge Buckley often found themselves traveling together between Rockledge and Denver. They had become well acquainted.

It was an acquaintance that worried defense attorneys like Amos P. Sharp, but there was nothing they could do about it.

When they climbed out of the stage coach in front of the Rockledge Hotel, Amos P. Sharp was there to meet them. Right then and there he asked for a hearing on a motion to dismiss criminal charges against James B. Casey. The judge said, "Very well," and set a hearing for the next day at 2 P.M.

* * *

The autopsy was finished. Dr. Benjamin Woodrow covered the body with a sheet and washed his hands in a pan of warm water in his kitchen. "She bled to death. She bled both externally and internally."

"Why did she do it?" Sheriff Jackson asked. "You said you warned her not to move, so why did she get out of bed and walk to the church, knowing it would kill her?"

"One can only speculate," Dr. Woodrow said. "She was not healing properly, and I had told her I might have to operate again."

Ruth Ann didn't have to speculate. "She wanted to die and she wanted to suffer doing it. What she and the reverend did must have been eating on her."

Sheriff Jackson said, "Well, she had to of suffered. It had to of been awful painful, what with the stitches tearing apart and hurting inside like that."

The discussion went on for a few minutes, then the outer door to the clinic opened. Jim Casey came in, rubbing his left shoulder. "I reckon," he said, "it's time to change the bandages." His eyes took in the linen-wrapped body on the examination table.

"Oh, of course," Ruth Ann said. "One moment, Mr. Casey."

"Jim. Call me Jim. Is that . . . is that Mrs. Mooreman?"

"Yes, Jim. She died last night."

"I heard. Lordy, I hope it wasn't . . . I went to her house yesterday and asked her some questions. I hope I didn't bring this on."

"No, Jim. She took her own life."

Casey swallowed a lump in his throat. "Lordy."

Having no other place to put the body at the moment, the doctor and the sheriff placed it on the floor in the doctor's office. Ruth Ann quickly washed the blood off

246

the table. "I know this isn't pleasant, Jim. You can sit in that chair if you'd rather."

Five men held a long conference in the sheriff's office. There were the defense lawyer, the prosecutor, the sheriff, his deputy, and Jim Casey. With only two chairs, all but the two attorneys leaned against the walls or sat on the floor.

"It sure looks bad for you Orville," Sheriff Jackson said to his deputy.

"I didn't do it."

"I wish I could agree with you, but look at the evidence. Your wife will have to admit under oath that she and the reverend were committing adultery. You found out, and you've been known to get fighting mad over your wife. You knocked her down and went home and thought about it. It ate on you, and you took that old Dragoon over there and went to the rectory to do what you believed any red-blooded man ought to do. When the shot was heard, a witness saw a man fitting your description running from the rectory."

"I don't care what it looks like, I didn't kill that man."

Sheriff Jackson asked the prosecutor, "What do you think?"

"If it can be proven that the deputy's wife was having an affair with the reverend, then circumstantial evidence points to him. But circumstantial evidence points to James Casey also."

"But," the defense lawyer put in, "the evidence against Deputy Rankin is as strong as the evidence against my client. The deputy had a motive. Some men would say it was a very strong motive. And when we impeach Agnes

Mooreman's testimony, the case against Deputy Rankin grows stronger."

Casey listened, but kept quiet.

Sheriff Jackson said, "Do you wanta go to trial, Orville? Have all your secrets told to the public?"

Deputy Rankin stomped across the room, turned, and stomped back, an angry scowl pulling his features together in a tight knot. "Rather than hang, yeah, damn right."

"You know what your wife will have to say under oath. You'll be made to look like a fool."

"Maybe she won't admit it. You can't prove it."

"She'll admit it. She'll admit it rather than go to jail for perjury. I don't think she could stand being locked up."

Rankin stomped across the room again. He stopped and faced the sheriff. "All right. I'll tell you what happened. I didn't shoot the son of a bitch." He paused, and the sheriff said softly, "What happened, Orville?"

"I went there to shoot 'im. I was so damned mad I couldn't think straight, and I took that old Dragoon and went over there to kill the son of a bitch." Another pause, then, "But when I got to the door I heard a shot from inside. I . . . I'm an officer of the law, and I should have gone in to see what happened. Instead, I stampeded. I guess I was afraid to be seen there in that frame of mind and with the Dragoon, and I just boogered and ran."

The prosecutor said, "You were so angry you were temporarily insane. Also, some jurors and jurists won't blame you. That will help in your sentencing."

"Perhaps not," Amos P. Sharp said. "He was in a murderous mood, but he had enough of his wits about him to use the old pistol instead of his own, thinking it might fool the investigators."

"God damn it, I did not do it." Deputy Rankin repeated himself in a loud angry voice. "I did not do it."

Casey had been squatting on his heels against a wall, not speaking. Now he stood and spoke calmly, quietly, "He didn't do it."

All eyes turned to him. Even the deputy stared at him, mouth open.

"The widow Mooreman did it."

"What?" Sheriff Jackson asked. "What in the holy hell makes you think so?"

"It just now came to me. I talked to her yesterday. There's a witness, Mrs. Gibbons who lives next door. What Agnes Mooreman said to me—with Mrs. Gibbons present—is pretty strong evidence."

Deputy Rankin asked, "Like what?"

"Here's what happened," Casey said, "Agnes Mooreman walked in on the reverend and Jennifer Rankin and caught them in bed. Until then, she thought the reverend was a saint. What they had between them was beautiful. Then everything blew up in her face. The saint turned out to be a sinner. In Mrs. Mooreman's own words, an adulterer.

"Now I'm not a mind reader, but I can guess how she felt. At first, she was stunned. She couldn't believe it. But after going home and thinking about it, the truth came to her. It hit her like a mule's kick. Everything she believed in had gone wrong." Casey paused, wanting to be sure of what he was saying.

Amos P. Sharp spoke up. "And right after Agnes Mooreman caught the two in bed and left, emotionally upset, Deputy Rankin went there and caught them in a compromising position, perhaps getting hastily dressed."

"Yeah," the deputy said. "I didn't see Agnes Mooreman leave, so I must of got there a few minutes after she left."

"That's what happened," Casey said. "And you know, when her husband was killed, when that freight wagon slipped off the jack and fell on him, all his belongings were given to the widow. His six-shooter was included. Old Whit carried that gun with every chamber loaded, and when they gave it to his widow, I'll bet nobody thought to unload it. The gun was in the house somewhere. She took it, hid it in her clothes, and went to the rectory. She put the gun within inches of Reverend Weem's chest and pulled the trigger. That was the shot Orville Rankin heard."

All were quiet. Then the prosecutor asked, "What do you think, Sheriff?"

"I'm inclined to believe it. It makes sense. I knew—I guess everybody knew by yesterday—that the widow Mooreman was making love with the reverend. She lied on the witness stand because she believed Jim here was the devil himself, and whatever he got he deserved. But when she found out she had a tumor and was facing surgery that could kill her she did a lot of praying in the church. Dr. Woodrow's assistant, Ruth Ann, thought she felt guilty about climbing into bed with the reverend. But now—after she admitted, according to Jim, that she knew the reverend was an adulterer—I'm beginning to believe she had more than that on her conscience. If the gun her late husband left her has been fired once, that's pretty good evidence she used it."

"And," the defense lawyer added, "her death last night was suicide."

"Yeah," the sheriff said. "Dr. Woodrow believes it was suicide, and I have to agree. She knew the truth was about to come out, and she wanted to die. Ruth Ann thinks she wanted to die in church, before the crucifix. It hurt like hell, getting out of bed and walking to the church, but the way Ruth Ann sees it, she wanted it that way. She pointed out that her Savior suffered when he died, and the widow Mooreman thought if she suffered, too, it would make it easier for her God to forgive her. It would cleanse her soul, is the way Ruth Ann put it."

Quiet again, then the prosecutor asked, "Can we get a statement from this Mrs. Gibbons?"

"Yes," said the defense lawyer. "She was a witness. She'll have to make a statement."

The sheriff said, "I'm gonna go to the dead woman's house and look for a gun. Anybody wanta go along?"

Everyone trooped to the house. In less than a minute, they found a pre-Civil War cap and ball six-gun in the bottom drawer of a dresser. They agreed that one shot had been fired from it. The gun hadn't been cleaned, and the expended percussion cap was still in place. "This's the way a woman would leave it," the sheriff said.

Somehow word got around, and sixteen spectators, including Mrs. Gibbons, were present in the courtroom when the prosecuting attorney told Judge Buckley about the new evidence. The judge readily complied with the attorney's motion to dismiss the murder charge against James B. Casey. As for the crime of jailbreak, Sheriff Jackson said he was willing to forget that, too. *Bang,* went the judge's gavel. "This case is dismissed," he said.

Amos P. Sharp shook hands with Jim Casey. The prosecutor, the sheriff, and two of the spectators joined in the handshaking. Everyone turned to leave.

Bang, went the gavel. "Ladies and gentlemen," Judge Buckley said, "I have another duty to perform in about—" he reached inside his robe for a gold-filled stemwinder watch—"in about two hours. I have a wedding to perform."

"Huh? Who's getting married?"

Reading from a sheet of paper on his desk, the judge said, "A Dr. Benjamin Woodrow and a Miss Ruth Ann Abraham. I have been informed that all interested parties are welcome."

A happy rumble went through the crowd. Everyone was smiling, talking and smiling. Someone said, "Wait 'till I tell my wife. She's gonna be tickled pink."

Sheriff Jackson grinned from ear to ear. "Now that's good news. That'll give this town something to be happy about."

From where he stood at the foot of his late wife's grave, Jim Casey was out of sight of Howdy, who was tearing down one side of a rotted corral, preparing to rebuild it. He was out of sight of the kitchen window. That was good. What he had to say was private. Head bowed, he spoke quietly:

"Well, Boots, we've lost some cattle and horses to the rustlers, and we'll have to sell a lot of cattle to pay off the bank and the lawyer. Me, I've been shot twice, and my left arm won't ever be the same. But don't worry now, I won't be crippled. It just won't be quite as strong as it used to be. We've still got our ranch, our land, and we'll restock. One thing about it, we won't overgraze this winter. But the best thing about all this is, I've found out we've got friends. Old Howell at the mercantile, Shipley at the bank, Dr. Woodrow and his assistant, now his wife. Even Sheriff Jackson. And old Levi and Mrs. Carter. They're the kind of people that keep this old world turning. We're lucky, Boots. We're darned lucky to have friends like them. Don't you worry about

Mrs. Carter and Levi, either. As long as we own this outfit, they won't have to work any more than they want to, and they'll always have a home. We owe it to them.

"Rest easy, my darlin'. We're just gonna keep on going."